MW01706157

FRONTIER'S CRUSADE

FRONTIERS BOOK 6

ROBERT C. JAMES

Cover design by Yvonne Less, Art 4 Artists

ONE

Hokkaido, Earth

Javier Petit had too much time on his hands. It was an odd sensation. One he'd rarely experienced.

In the reflection of the mirror, he couldn't get over how tired the man staring back at him was. The grays had begun streaking through his hair decades ago. But he never felt old. He'd been too fixated on his work to ever stop to think about his mortality. Life was just too short. But with everything that had happened of late, with the discovery of the Retebu sphere on Orion V, the adventures on the *Cargo Ship Argo*, and the opening of the gateway to Alliance space, something inside him was finally pulling him back.

Others had told him to slow down for as long as he could remember, but he never took notice of them. His existence would be but a pinprick on the galactic time-line, and he had too much to achieve before his light was extinguished.

But with an internal force now fighting against him, he had no choice but to take heed. Strangely, he decided to listen to that voice, and left his home in the city, informing the Tokyo Institute of Advanced Sciences that he'd be taking a sabbatical from his work at the place he'd called home since he was a much younger man.

Javier stepped to the window of his log-style cabin on the hillside of the lush greenery of Hokkaido and rested his arms against the sill, breathing in the crisp morning air. Whenever he peered out upon his surroundings, he imagined himself as a child up in a treehouse. The height in which his house was nestled was both magical and a little disconcerting all at the same time.

He turned and picked up his coffee from the kitchen counter and walked into his makeshift laboratory. While he was no longer under the official eye of TIAS, he still couldn't stop himself persisting with his theoretical work. Though, as he scrutinized the blackboards filling every wall and all the papers strewn over his desk, he couldn't help but feel his talents were being wasted. Javier always liked to get his hands dirty. Theoretical work was fine, but it was the 'doing' that you really discovered the secrets of the universe.

He grabbed a series of data tablets from his chair and plonked them on top of another pile of papers on his desk. He then took a seat and rested his stiff muscles. With a sip of his coffee, he let the heat fill his insides and did his best to feel at ease.

A bird chirped beyond his window, and he leaned

over. A slight breeze kicked up, unsettling the papers in his office, and the bird chirped again. He focused in on the tallest tree on his property, and the tiny creature stared back at him.

Javier had seen many birds in his short time in Hokkaido and recognized a lot of the different varieties. But he didn't recognize his latest visitor. It almost seemed to be a Eurasian Wryneck, which was native to his motherland, France. And while it was well-traveled, he'd never known it to settle in the north of Japan.

Javier reached for his bird-watching book, teetering on the edge of the desk, and snatched it, just before his movement sent it careening to the floor. He opened the text devoted to the Hokkaido region and flicked through it from front to back. He was right. The Wryneck wasn't a local of his new home. The bird continued to eye him and even moved closer to his window.

"So where are you from, little one?" Javier whispered, not wanting to spook it. He returned his book to his cluttered desk and stretched for a fresh notepad to take down its characteristics.

Then his doorbell rang.

Javier dropped his pad, surprised by the noise. The Wryneck, too startled, lifted off and flew away into the deep beyond of the Hokkaido forest. Javier closed his eyes in frustration and wondered who could be at his front door.

He moved his weary bones and made his way to the wooden door that divided the warm confines of his treetop home to the elements of the cool Japanese winter. With a twist of the handle, he pulled it ajar to find a slender man standing in front of him.

But he wasn't a man. At least not a human one.

"Professor Petit?"

Javier didn't know what to say as he peered out at the lumpy-skinned extraterrestrial, with small orange eyes and an extremely thin layer of dark hair. The yellow and green hue of his skin almost glowed in the morning sun. "Uh, yes, that's me."

A smile appeared on the alien's face. "Good, I've come a long way."

"I can only imagine."

"My name is Garin Onlor. I'm here today to request an audience."

Javier raised his eyebrows, flattered but wary at the same time. He gestured inside, and Onlor took the invitation to enter. The pair walked into the living area, which was the perfect vantage point to enjoy the majestic scenery around his home. "You're the first person who's visited me since my move from Tokyo."

Onlor sat on the sofa against the wall. "I find that hard to believe."

Javier also sat, taking the sofa opposite. "I had explicit instructions that during my sabbatical that no one disturb me."

"I apologize, Professor, but it was of the utmost importance I see you in person." Onlor leaned forward. "I couldn't ask you over a commlink."

"Ask me what?"

"You remember the Kalceni base the CDF expeditionary fleet discovered in the Kappa-Magellan star system, prior to their weapon ship's attack on the Alliance."

"Of course. I was a part of the expeditionary fleet." Javier shifted uncomfortably. "I see it in my dreams and my nightmares whenever I go to sleep."

"That's understandable." Onlor sat back, though the muscles in his arms were still tense. "I myself have never visited. After the Kalcenis' destruction, the Alliance put a temporary ban on anyone visiting Kappa-Magellan. Many in the Alliance Council were rattled at what it represented, and what remained there. But those in the Alliance's scientific sphere have finally convinced them of the need to study it. I work for the Company who you've had dealings with in the past. The council have decided to send us in, and I'm to head the expedition."

Javier tapped at the arm of the sofa. "And you've come here today to ask me for my notes on the Kalceni station?"

"No, I want more than that." Onlor put his hands together and coughed but swiftly pushed aside the dryness of his throat. "I want you to come with me, Professor."

"Me?" Javier was almost lost for words. The haunting images of the inside of the station appeared in his mind, along with the destruction caused by the weapon ship that pierced the heart of the Alliance. "It's a flattering invitation, but as you can see, I'm winding down."

"I understand that, Professor, but we all get one calling in life. Exploration is the center of everything we do. And there's only so much one can do sitting inside four walls. Your species, as much as mine and any other throughout the universe, were destined to fly. You belong out there, not in here."

Javier peered past Onlor through the window and swore he caught a glimpse of the little bird who had visited him earlier. But as quickly as it had come, it disappeared.

He returned his attention to his visitor and shook his head with a wry smile. "When do we leave?"

TWO

Cargo Ship Argo

Jason Cassidy opened his eyes, and the glow from the ship parked next to the *Argo* in the huge hangar deck of Myjurna Station lit up his quarters.

He didn't remember falling asleep with it so bright so assumed its crew must have activated their running lights, readying for departure. As with all the other spacecrafts docked in the alien station, it made the *Argo* seem like an exhibit from a museum. It was the same in most places in Alliance space they visited. All the other vessels were constructed with more advanced techniques and higher quality materials. Jason chuckled to himself thinking about his trip to Psi-Aion. It felt like an eternity ago, when the thought of meeting an extraterrestrial seemed outlandish.

How times change...

Back on Psi-Aion, they were the higher form of life, at least when compared to the natives of the gorgeous green world. The inhabitants there at one point even assumed Jason was a god. Now the shoe was well and truly on the other foot as they earned a crust on the opposite side of the gateway, traveling amongst the stars. He wondered what others thought when they saw the *Argo* and his crew. Did they see a rickety old wooden raft and ancient Neanderthals like they had on Psi-Aion?

A hand reached from behind him and placed itself on his shoulder.

"Hey," a soft voice called out to him.

Jason fell back into his pillow and rested his head next to Aly Rycroft as she awakened from her slumber. "Well, good morning, Miss Rycroft," he said, leaning in for a kiss which she immediately returned.

She ruffled her blonde bed hair about and yawned, taking a peek through the viewport. "Seems our neighbors are leaving."

"Appears so."

And as if right on cue, the alien vessel lifted off, retracting its landing struts and pushing past them through the hangar deck doors into open space.

Aly pulled herself up. "You're deep in thought."

"Not really." Jason fluffed his pillow and dragged it up so he could sit beside her with the help of the bulkhead behind him. He looked up at the bare wall, remembering the days when Sky Jensen and Anabelle Pearl stared down at him. The posters had been stuck there since his teenage years, but he felt the time had come to take them down. It just wasn't appropriate anymore, considering he'd been sharing his quarters with Aly for the past six months.

"Ugh, I should get up." Aly tugged the cover over her face. "But I don't want to."

Jason glanced at the chronometer on his commband sitting on the bedside table.

"Then don't," he said. "It's not even seven a.m."

"There's so much I need to do in the engine room. That trip we took near the Ventris Cluster played havoc with our FTL systems."

"We got here in one piece." Jason shrugged. "And we got the shipment delivered on time. We're in no rush. It's still two days until our new shipment arrives, and then we don't need to set off for another three days, considering how quickly the gateways can take us to Vantar."

"True, but you know me, I like to get things done. And if I let it linger, it'll play on my mind."

"I could order you to stay in bed." Jason wrapped his arms around her and drew her closer to him. "You know I'm captain of this ship, right?"

She leaned in and kissed him again, placing her arms over his shoulders. Then Jason's commband bleeped.

The pair pulled away from one another and rolled their eyes.

"I don't have to answer it," he said.

It bleeped again, and Aly reached over him to grab the commband. She activated it and held it in front of his mouth.

"This is Jason." He gritted his teeth. "Go ahead."

"I need you in the infirmary," Kevin said over the channel.

"Why?"

"There's been an accident."

Jason and Aly quickly got dressed and rushed from their quarters up to A Deck and through the door into the infirmary. There standing over the main bed was Aly's father, Kevin Rycroft, and lying on the bed, Conrad Althaus. His half-uncle's teeth were gnashed together and his cheeks almost a crimson red.

"What happened?" Jason asked, approaching to find Althaus's right leg nearly ninety degrees out of place. "Holy crap!"

The bone-setter, around his leg, cracked and crunched until it was back in its rightful position.

"To hell with it!" Althaus yelled out in agony as he balled his hands into fists.

Kevin waved a medical scanner over it and with a satisfied nod, peeled the bone-setter off him and put it on the tray beside the bed. He then attached a self-wrapping cast, which wound its way from the knee to the ankle.

"More drugs, Rycroft!" Althaus demanded.

Kevin checked what he had in the many cabinets and found a packet of pills and something to inject him with. He stabbed the medicine into Althaus's arm and handed him the tablets. "Every four hours you can take two."

"How about you just give me a few more of those

hypodermics instead?" A grogginess started to take hold of the patient, and he grabbed at the hypodermic in Kevin's hand. But he missed, and Kevin set it down on the medical tray.

"How did he do this?" Jason asked.

"He was down in the cargo bay making room for the next shipment, moving a hover lifter into an empty space. It malfunctioned. The engine failed, and it fell on him. It broke his leg instantly in two places, but the stubborn bull he is wedged himself free, doing even more damage higher toward the knee."

Jason peered down at Althaus, and his uncle looked into his eyes. The irate man had all but disappeared and was replaced with a medicated drunk. "Will it heal?"

"He'll be fine," Kevin assured him.

"How long?"

"I've injected him with self-healing nanites which will speed up the process. I should be able to take the cast off in the next two weeks. Until then, he won't be doing anything."

"Very well. I guess we'll just have to pick up the slack." He stopped himself before giving Althaus a ribbing. It wasn't the man's fault he'd got injured. "Can you check out that hover lifter, Aly?"

She nodded and rushed out of the infirmary, leaving the three men on their own. Althaus's eyes started to close, and his head fell back into his pillow as the drugs took hold.

Jason put his hands on his hips. "We've had problems with those lifters before. Usually, they warn you before they fail."

Kevin shrugged. "It might have been a significant fault. I guess those things are pretty old now. Or it could have been something else."

Jason raised his eyebrows. "Something else?"

"Perhaps it's not just the hover lifter that's getting old."

Jason returned his focus Althaus. He began snoring, and drool ran from the corner of his mouth. Jason had always seen the man as the epitome of strength. One that seemed like an immovable wall, especially when Jason was a child. But in that moment, the bald head, and a body that was more fat than muscle these days, encapsulated what Father Time had done to his uncle. "Sometimes I wish I could go back to being a kid. You, Althaus, Dad—"

"Time waits for no one. The god or gods, or whoever is watching over us, take as quickly as they give." Kevin packed up the medical equipment he had left over and stored it away, while disposing of everything else. "We just have to make do with what we're given and enjoy it while we can, because once it's over..."

Jason let Kevin's philosophy lesson fade away while he walked to the other side of the infirmary. He thought back to his earliest memories on the *Argo* and worried at how many of them he still remembered.

THREE

Aly walked from the engine room, wiping her hands with her favorite rag. Though she cleaned it regularly, it had become as black as the inside of the *Argo's* FTL engines. She couldn't even remember what color it started out as.

She laced it through her belt and headed to the galley for a drink. The water from the tap was especially fresh after such a hard morning of work. She knocked back two full glasses then made a beeline for her quarters. But she stopped herself before entering, remembering it was no longer her home. At least not for the last six months.

Moving in with Jason had been a huge change. When he'd asked her to move in, she was hesitant at first. But it made the most sense considering his quarters were slightly larger than the space she'd grown up in. They'd talked about shifting their belongings into Benjamin Cassidy's old quarters, which were even bigger, but something didn't sit right with either of them doing that.

Aly was about to continue onward, when a bang sounded beyond the door. She pushed the door ajar to find Jason sitting on his lonesome behind the shabby desk they'd found in storage. When they'd agreed to move into his quarters, they'd also decided to use her former space as an office. With all the work they'd picked up, Jason thought the time was right to have a pseudo-admin area to deal with their business affairs.

A small computer sat on the desk connected to the *Argo's* main systems, and sprawled over it were a stack of data tablets, all starting to pile up. Jason glanced up at her as she entered. His stare hadn't changed since learning of Althaus's broken leg.

"You look frustrated," she said.

"That would be an understatement." He held up one of the tablets. "I've often wondered how much Althaus actually does around here, but after checking over the jobs we've done in the six months since the Centauri incident, it really is amazing what he does to keep us chugging along."

"More than just a grouchy old man, huh?"

"Something like that." Jason chuckled. "Luckily, he's already set up our next shipment, because with all the networking he's done, it'd be hard to get my head around everything. And then to top it off, he has the cargo bay in order twenty-four hours a day, and ready for any contingencies. Between that and this paperwork, I'm really not looking forward to the next few weeks."

Aly grabbed the tablet from him and placed it on the desk. "Come on, let's go."

"Where are we going?" he asked.

"For a walk."

He shook his head. "I shouldn't. I've—"

Aly took his hand and pulled him to his feet. "I'm going for a stroll around the station and I need my man to escort me."

Jason smiled and relented, leaving his pile of work behind him. They left the *Argo* and made their way through the expansive landing bay to the inner corridors of Myjurna Station. Apart from a quick glimpse of the place on the day they'd landed, it was the first proper visit Aly had taken of the facility. She couldn't recall stopping over at another facility quite as big. It was double the size of the Valkeris Station in orbit of Tadrosia, and ten times bigger than Odyssey Station.

Aly couldn't forget the moment she'd met Jason for the first time since he'd left the *Argo* to go to the academy and become an officer in the CDF. He appeared different. He acted different. But somewhere inside him was the real Jason Cassidy that she knew and loved. She peered across at him as they stepped into the huge bazaar where alien races of all kinds went about their business, trading and exchanging goods.

They continued through the bustling marketplace and strolled to an upper deck filled with shop fronts, more akin to a galactic shopping center. Jason stopped at one that seemed rather innocuous, but when Aly had a good peek inside, she quickly understood it was anything but.

"Let's go," he told her.

Aly grasped his hand tight. "We don't travel the galaxy to frequent every bar we come across."

"Why else do we do it?" Jason said with a cheeky grin. "Come on. One drink."

She shook her head, trying to hide her frustration, and followed him into the busy establishment. The same mix of species from earlier sat at the bar and the surrounding tables, drinking some of the more bizarre concoctions she'd seen. Jason led her to the bar, and a fat orange alien marched toward them from the other side of it.

"What would you like?" he said, in a tone so deep Aly thought his voice might shake the station around them.

Jason eyed her.

"I'll have a water," she said.

"And you?" the alien asked.

Jason peered at all the different bottles on the wall of the bar, licking his lips. He then glanced back at Aly and smiled. "Make it two."

The orange alien went to the dispenser behind him. "Right. Two waters."

Aly raised her eyebrows. "You know you could have had a drink."

He shrugged. "I guess I just wasn't quite thirsty for that at the moment."

The barman plonked the large triangular glasses of

water in front of them and turned without saying a word, though his indignance was loud and clear.

Jason took a sip of his beverage. "I've been thinking about things this morning."

"Oh?" she said.

"Yeah. With Althaus out of commission for at least the next two weeks, I think now might be the time to get some help."

Aly gazed off at nothing in particular, remembering when she was briefly in charge of the *Argo* and had similar thoughts. Back then it would have been difficult because of their lack of funds, but their fortunes had changed. "I guess we have the money now, don't we? We've built a nice little surplus for ourselves."

Jason nodded. "We could easily afford someone. Apparently, there's a hire agency right here on Myjurna."

"So, we'd be just replacing him for two weeks?"

"Maybe." Jason took another swig of his water. "What if they were half decent? We've always said four crew members wasn't going to work forever, especially with all the business we've come into lately."

"I agree." She nodded. "It'll sure be weird having someone else on the ship, though."

"I know. But we have to move with the times." He finished his drink and put it in front of him. "I'll get onto the agency later and see what we can set up."

Someone bumped into Jason's back, forcing the glass over the edge. It shattered right behind the barman, who turned and glared at him.

"Hey!"

Jason swiveled on his barstool to a green alien with a harsh brow and piercing eyes. Not to mention at least a couple of feet taller.

"You got in my way!" he growled.

"I was just sitting here!" Jason shot back.

He hauled Jason by the scruff of the neck and pulled him from the stool, lifting his feet from the deck. "Don't talk back to me, little man."

Aly grabbed at the alien's arms but could barely grasp the sheer muscles surrounding his bones.

"I think you should let me go," Jason said calmly, not letting the huge being see his fear.

Everyone in the bar stopped what they were doing and stared in their direction.

The alien laughed. "You are a pathetic thing, aren't you?"

"Maybe, but at least I've got a good kick on me." Jason swung his right leg out and booted the aggressor between the legs.

But the alien didn't flinch. Not even a little.

Jason glanced at Aly with his eyes as wide as saucers. "Ah, crap!"

FOUR

"Wrong choice!"

The alien aggressor laughed and heaved Jason above his head, tossing him over the bar, careening into the mirror on the back wall. The bottles of liquor smashed to the floor and crashed around him as the artificial gravity of the station splattered him down on his face.

He rolled onto his back, grimacing at the impact of the thud and the cuts on his arms from the broken glass. The alien reached for him again, but Jason quickly scrambled on his knees, finding half a bottle within his grasp. He clutched it and stabbed it into the alien's arm.

His attacker groaned out, but the pain lasted mere moments. The gash to his green skin only made him angrier. He swatted the bottle from Jason's hand and dragged him back over the bar. He then flung him to the other side of the establishment into a table, breaking it in two and scattering the chairs around it. Everyone else moved toward the outer wall and continued to watch on.

Jason slowly got himself to his feet, gasping for air, and peered across at Aly who was being held with her arms behind her back by the alien's smaller but just as intimidating friends.

Jason grabbed the closest chair to him and held it with the legs pointing outward. The alien came at him again, and he backed up as far as the crowd would let him.

The alien lunged, but Jason dodged and pushed the chair toward him. He got a few whacks in, but they didn't even register a grunt from the larger-bodied being. He swatted at Jason and yanked the chair from his hands, breaking it into tiny pieces and throwing it at the crowd.

Jason saw his chance and dove under the alien's legs, sliding to the other end of the bar to prep himself for another onslaught. Beyond, Aly resisted the handling of the other aliens, but her nuggety fight was in vain against the stronger beings. She and Jason locked eyes with each other. Both knew there was little he could do. Not until he'd dispatched the guy trying to bury him six feet under.

"Come here, you pathetic piece of slabgotcsch!" The huge alien came for Jason again and backed him into the corner. He had nowhere to go, and the alien picked him up again, lifting him to his eyeline. The attacker's red eyes glared at him, and his breath reeked like the bathroom on the *Argo* after one of Althaus's famed chili nights.

"I think we got off on the wrong foot," Jason said,

knowing that his fate was likely sealed. He didn't care so much for his safety but for Aly's. "Perhaps if we just sat down and—"

"Quiet!" he yelled, with a breath so harsh it made Jason's hair blow up as if he was caught in a strong wind.

"Why don't you pick on someone your own size?"

Everyone in the bar turned to a short alien woman with black hair in a ponytail, making her way through the crowd and stopping in the middle of what had become a fighting ring. The green aggressor stared her down and dropped Jason in the process. He moved toward her as Jason pulled himself to his feet.

The dark-haired alien, who was even shorter than Aly, squared up with the hulking giant. The pair stepped around each other, and then out of nowhere the woman leaped in the air and kicked the big goon in the head. The shock of the blow drove him backward, nearly taking out a section of the onlookers.

She didn't let him get comfortable and went at him again, whacking him from the other side, with a firm combination of punches to his head. He tried to lunge at her, but she ducked and swept at his legs, forcing him down like a collapsing building.

Jason saw his chance and sped toward the aliens holding on to Aly. He jumped in the air and kicked one in the chest, pushing them over the top of the bar.

The other one let Aly go and swung his right fist at Jason, planting a punch to his head and knocking him over.

Aly, unencumbered, took hold of him from behind, getting her own revenge and wrapping her arms around his neck and dragging him backward to the floor.

The rattled alien from the other side of the bar got up. Jason spotted him out of the corner of his eye and snatched an empty bottle and unleashed it across his forehead, sending him crashing back down.

The other alien got himself up and rushed toward Aly, but Jason tackled him before he could get his hands on her, pile-driving him into the hard deck.

He spun him around and punched him in the face until his eyes tired. Aly tugged Jason by the arm to stop him from going any harder, and they turned to the fight still taking place over from them.

The green alien cornered the small woman near the far wall. She glanced back at the ever-approaching wall and jumped up it, almost breaking the laws of physics. Gravity eventually brought her down, right on top of her opponent.

She hooked her arms around his neck, and he bucked like a raging bull. He tried swatting her away, but she was too quick for him, dodging his menacing swings. She kneed him in the spine and punched him repeatedly in the neck.

He spun around and fell to the floor, shaking the deck in the process. He attempted to get back up, but she grasped his head with both her hands and smashed it into the deck.

Again and again.

Blood splattered from his cut forehead, and the green goliath groaned out until he simply gave up.

Jason and Aly stood across from her between all the carnage, and the trio locked eyes.

Then from out of nowhere, the local authorities started barreling through the crowd. The petite alien savior made a run for it, while everyone in the bar scrambled for the exits.

Jason clutched Aly by the hand and followed them out.

Cargo Ship Argo

"What were you thinking getting into a bar brawl?"

Kevin ran a handheld skin regenerator over Jason's face, which was covered in bruises and cuts. They all hurt, along with the rest of the wounds that had been inflicted on his body at the hands of the hulking green alien on Myjurna Station.

"It's not like we had much of a choice," Aly said to her father, with plenty of her own bruises from the scuffle.

"So, this wasn't one of those instances where you were defending her honor?" Kevin asked.

Jason chuckled. "Not this time."

Kevin took some ointment from his tray and rubbed it into the freshly healed skin on Jason's forehead.

"The problem you've got is you can't punch your way out of a brown paper bag."

Everyone turned to Althaus walking into the infirmary on a pair of crutches to support his broken appendage.

Jason rolled his eyes. "If you'd have been there, he would've snapped more than your legs."

"I'd have made a good fight of it, at least. I have a lot of tricks up my sleeve."

"That's because you're a dirty fighter."

"To be fair," Aly interjected, "you tried to kick him in the nuts."

"If you're going to do it, you have to know where their nuts are," Althaus added with a smirk.

"Next time I'll make sure to brush up on my opponent's anatomy." Jason winced at the sting of the ointment and waved Kevin's hand away.

Althaus left the infirmary, no doubt believing his work was done.

Aly shook her head, unable to hide her own smile. "The more things change, the more they stay the same."

Kevin finished working on Jason and handed him some pills. "These aren't as good as the stuff I gave Althaus, but they should do the job if the pain gets worse." He then glanced at his daughter. "Luckily, you're not as bad, so you should be fine without anything. I'm sure looking after him will be pain enough."

Jason hopped off the bed, and Aly wrapped an arm around his waist.

"Be gentle with him," her dad said, shaking his head as the pair made their way to the exit.

FIVE

Alpha Station

Javier disembarked his transport craft from the surface of Earth and walked out into the station's major terminal. A frenzy of activity welcomed him aboard the enormous facility which had become more of a civilian hub since the construction of the gateway.

He hadn't visited the installation since the doorway to the rest of the galaxy went online and the first ships sailed through it to Alliance space. It was then that he started thinking about winding back on his work. Not long after that he went back to TIAS and informed them of his decision to take a sabbatical.

One major change that had taken place in his absence was how much busier it had gotten. No doubt with the Centauri incident now in the past, and relations with the Alliance more settled, traffic was again picking up and people were feeling more at ease at traveling through the gateway.

Javier heaved his luggage onto his manual trolley while the rest of the passengers from his transport nudged him along. He found himself stuck in the crowd connecting the various gates, so he quickly discovered a path to safety, pushing onward and stopping by a large viewport.

Beyond it lay the massive gateway and the blue jewel of Earth below. To this day, whenever he saw the structure, a sense of pride overcame him. He'd been the driver behind many significant advances during his lifetime, no more notable than the Mark IV FTL drive. But as he stared out at the gateway, he knew he'd always hold a special place for the program which led to its creation. In reality it had been little more than a flat-pack construction, but what it signified for humanity could never be forgotten.

He placed his hand on the viewport and closed his eyes, trying to filter out the noise around him. There was something so disconcerting about the thousands of passenger's voices melding together as one. Either he was getting older quicker than he'd thought, or the time spent in his temporary home in Hokkaido had gotten him more accustomed to the quieter life.

The whir of a small engine closed behind him, and he opened his eyes to the familiar sound. He pulled his hand from the window and straightened his back.

"Hello, Javier."

He pricked up his ears at the voice. It too was very familiar, and he turned to find Doctor Susan Tai sitting in her mobility chair behind him.

"Well, well," he said. "Someone obviously did a better job than me getting through that crowd."

"I don't give them a choice. I may not have a cow-catcher on this thing, but it does the job." She smirked and gestured toward the viewport. "Checking out your handiwork?"

"Once upon a time, I would have said yes. You know how vain I am."

Susan chuckled and moved her chair beside him so they could both gaze at the gateway. "Last I heard, you'd left TIAS to explore your inner self."

"Is that what they told you? Our colleagues at the Institute must have thought long and hard to come up with that one." Javier frowned. "No, it's got nothing to do with that, it's just—"

Susan put up her hand. "You don't have to explain it to me."

"You're a wonderful friend, Susan."

"We've been through so much." She glanced at his bags. "I gather you're heading on a trip."

"Uh, yes." He took hold of his heavy trolley, stacked tall with his luggage. "The Company have invited me on an expedition."

"Sounds exciting."

"Well..."

Susan raised an eyebrow.

"I'm returning to the Kalceni base in the Kappa-Magellan system."

Her brow rose even higher. "Well, I'm glad it's you and not me. How did they talk you into that?"

"I honestly don't know."

"What do the Company expect to find there?"

"I suppose they want to investigate the technology the Kalceni have left behind. I guess the Company figure we should be ready for them."

"Well, I for one hope they're as dead as that weapon ship. I don't think any amount of investigation could prepare us for them again."

Javier couldn't disagree. But he'd devoted his life to study. It's what he knew and what he did best. "Anyway, I never got to congratulate you on your work discovering the cure to Jung's Disease. It's a remarkable achievement."

"Thank you." She paused for a moment, and her gaze lingered somewhere beyond. "There were a few hiccups in the trial stages, but we're finally ready to roll out the vaccine. With any luck, within the next twelve months no one else will ever have to bear the burden of that horrible disease."

"Nicolas would be proud of you." Javier cursed under his breath mentioning her dead husband's name. "I'm sorry, Susan. I didn't mean—"

"Please, Javier." She smiled in a manner he hadn't seen in some time. "I've come a long way since..."

She drifted off, and Javier caught a glimpse of the auto hover lifter stacked with bags behind her.

"I see I'm not the only one going on a trip," he said.

"Yes, well, I'm heading through the gateway, too."

"Destination?"

"I promised myself once the cure to the disease had been found, I'd go back to regain my legs."

Javier took Susan's hand again and squeezed it tight. "I'm so happy for you."

She nodded as an alien transport ship emerged from the gateway. "Hopefully I'll remember how to use them."

"It's probably just like riding a bike."

"Can Professor Petit report to gate thirty-five? This is a call for Professor Petit to gate thirty-five," a voice rang out over the speakers throughout the terminal.

Some people in the crowd of passengers stopped what they were doing, no doubt recognizing the name, while most others simply carried on rushing toward whatever destination they were heading to.

"It would seem your chariot awaits," Susan said.

"Seems so." He released her hand. "I guess it wouldn't be too professional to be tardy, would it?"

"I don't think they'll go without you." Susan looked over his bags on the old-style trolley. "Don't rush. Make sure you and everything else gets there in one piece."

Javier leaned over and hugged her, feeling a twinge in his lower back. "Once we've both returned to Earth, how about we find a park somewhere in Tokyo and take a walk like we used to?"

"How about Hokkaido instead?"

"Hokkaido it is." Javier grabbed his trolley and lugged his bags through the busy epicenter of Alpha Station until he finally made it to gate thirty-five and the airlock to Onlor's ship.

A male Ulvekan, the same species as Onlor, put out a hand, inviting him on board. He even took the awkward trolley for him, leading him through the airlock and onto the Company vessel. The soft gray corridors were welcoming, and the cosmopolitan crew, who walked by him, smiled at him as they passed.

Javier's escort handed off the trolley to a younger crewmember and motioned for him to enter an elevator. It shot up the shaft, traversing several decks in a matter of seconds. The doors slid open, and Javier stepped out onto the bridge. There waiting at the rear on a platform overlooking the main station was the man who had come asking for his help in Japan.

The alien was deep in conversation with a subordinate until he spotted Javier. He immediately shooed away the underling and waved for Javier to come up the steps to the platform. "Welcome aboard the *Brielaro*, Professor, I'm glad you could join us."

Javier climbed the platform and stood beside the tall Ulvekan, taking hold of the handrail. "It's an honor to be here."

With the formalities over with, Onlor directed his helmsman to depart. The *Brielaro* detached from Alpha Station and turned toward the gateway.

"Are you ready, Professor?" the expedition leader asked.

Javier took a deep breath. "Ready as I'll ever be."

Onlor grinned and approached his helmsman. Before them, a trans-space corridor appeared at the heart of the gateway, inviting them inside.

SIX

"So, tell me again, why you left your last job?"

Jason looked up from the data tablet in his makeshift office, while Aly creaked her chair beside him. Their interviewee, a short Grenoian with enormous arms and legs, resembled an old wooden barrel with limbs.

Kraun scratched his sparsely covered head of hair. "I won't lie to you. On the last cargo ship I worked on, I got into a few disagreements with some of my shipmates."

"What kind of disagreements?" Aly asked.

"All kinds, really. I guess they just had personalities that didn't gel with mine."

"Did you find this happened on most of your jobs?"

"From time to time."

Jason glanced ever so subtly out the corner of his eye at Aly, who returned the hint of bemusement. "It says here that you've been in logistics for the past two hundred and ten years."

"What can I say? I love the work."

"And going off your résumé, you average a new job every six months. That's a lot."

Kraun shrugged. "I go where I have to, to earn a crust."

"We might be wanting someone long-term, is that something you'd be prepared for?" Aly said, taking the tablet from Jason and perusing it for herself.

"If you pay me, you've got me for as long as you want."

Jason drummed his fingers against the desk, and silence permeated throughout Aly's old quarters. "We'll check through our notes on everyone we've interviewed today and get back to you."

Kraun stood, no doubt a little taken aback by how short the interview was. One of his fists clenched into a ball, just before he could hide it behind his back. Through gritted teeth he nodded and turned, walking out the door and clanging it shut behind him.

Aly threw the tablet on the desk with the others, and Jason shook his head. "That's the seventeenth person we've interviewed," he said.

"Eighteenth, actually," she corrected him.

"What kind of agency are they running here? There hasn't been one who's come along that's even remotely suitable to work on the *Argo*."

"Well, Kraun has a lot of experience."

"I'm not hiring an alien version of Althaus. I'd much prefer someone that won't punch me in the back of the head when I give them an order they don't like."

Aly picked up another tablet from the stack. "What about Hidurna? He seemed okay."

"You mean the one who was the only survivor of a ship where all the airlocks had been blown? The one where three hundred and sixty-four other crew members were found floating through space? That one?"

She chuckled. "What about Lohtahki?"

Jason scratched his head and yanked the tablet from her hand to check through the names. He quickly passed it back to her. "You're talking about the guy who was even more busted up than Althaus. And he had three legs, not to mention a third eye. I swear it didn't stop looking at me the whole time he was in here."

"But he was really nice."

"Nice won't cut it."

"But you don't want a jackass either?"

"I just want someone competent. And normal."

She scoured their notes again. "I'm not sure what to tell you, but I don't think we're going to find anyone here."

A knock sounded at the door, and it swung slightly ajar.

Kevin peeked his head inside. "Are you two free?"

Jason waved him in. "What is it?"

"There's someone here to see you." Kevin stood aside, and behind him their alien savior from the bar came into view.

She didn't seem as fierce as the last time they'd seen her, but she still appeared just as forthright with a ramrod-straight back and a stare that didn't waver.

"This is Mirin," Kevin said, introducing her. "I found her outside the rear entry ramp. She, uh, asked to see you."

"It's nice to meet you." Jason stood. "We had hoped to thank you for your help yesterday, but you were in quite a rush after your victory over Godzilla."

"The Myjurnans aren't too fond of people making a mess of their station," she said. "It was best for all of us to make a quick getaway."

"Well, for what it's worth, even if it's a little late, thank you. If you hadn't come when you had, I hate to think what that thing would have done to us."

"Oh, I assure you he would have eventually pulled off all your limbs and disemboweled you."

Silence lingered in the office, and Kevin made his way into the B Deck corridor. "If you need me, I'll be in the galley."

He closed the door behind him, and Mirin approached the desk, handing Jason a data tablet.

"You probably want to know why I'm here," she said. "My last job fell through, and I'm searching for work. I wasn't able to apply quick enough through the agency for the position aboard your ship, so I decided to take a more direct route."

Jason took the tablet and read her résumé, sitting back down. "So, you're not only handy with your fists but quite the cargo jockey as well."

"I've worked in over fifty star systems, on small ships and big. All my references are there. I think you'll find everything is in order."

Jason passed the tablet to Aly. "What skills can you bring to the *Argo*?"

"You're after someone to take care of your cargo bay. I can do that. You need someone to work with traders. I've built up a network that would see you with plentiful jobs for the foreseeable future. I'm also pretty handy with a spanner."

Aly glanced up from the résumé. "You know your way around an engine room?"

"I'm not a fully qualified engineer, but I've learned a lot over the years. Your *Argo* isn't anywhere near as advanced as the other ship's I've worked on, so I shouldn't have a problem coming up to speed here."

Jason caught Aly's glare at the other woman, but it quickly subsided.

"I could always use an extra pair of hands around here," she said, putting the tablet down. "Are you comfortable with the rate of pay we're offering?"

"It's a little less than I normally take, but if you give me a cut of every job I find, that should more than account for what I'm after."

Jason tapped his fingers on the desk, leaving a mark in the shoddy fake wood finish. "We've seen a lot of people today. You'll understand we've got much to talk through."

"Of course," Mirin said.

"Leave it with us, and we'll get back to you by the end of the day with our decision."

Aly returned the data tablet to Mirin, who made her way to the exit.

"Oh, one more thing," Jason said before she walked out. "Where did you learn to fight like that?"

"My home world," she replied.

"Which is where?"

"A...very long way from here." Mirin turned and traipsed over the threshold, closing the door softly behind her.

Aly stacked all the tablets in a neat pile. "Well, what do you think?"

"What do I think?" Jason leaned back in his chair. "It goes without saying that she was the best one to walk through that door all day."

"But?"

He laughed, humored by how well Aly could read him. "I guess I'm just trying to get past the fact we're about to finally have a crew member on this ship that isn't a Cassidy, Rycroft, or an Althaus. It's been a very long time."

Aly took his hand. "You know it's the right decision to make."

Jason stared into nothingness, with the image of the crippled Althaus inside the infirmary lingering on his mind.

"Yeah, I guess it is." He scrounged for his comm-band on the far side of the desk and activated it. "Jason to Kevin."

"Kevin here. Go ahead," Aly's father replied over the *Argo's* internal commlink.

"If you're between coffees, can you do me a favor and find Mirin before she leaves the ship?"

"Oh?"

"Yeah." Jason smiled at Aly. "I think we've found our new crewmember."

SEVEN

Mirin strode up the rear entry ramp of the very odd-looking ship, with all her belongings in a bag hanging over her right shoulder.

The *Argo* was so old compared to anything she'd ever seen. Though she was hardly surprised. The development of the human species was unique, with their home world located on the far side of the ancient Kalceni-Retebu battleground known to them as Frontier's Reach. Naturally, everything to do with them would be quite different to those that developed in the Alliance.

She almost envied the humans. Very few worlds got to make contact with the wider galactic neighborhood at such a high level of their development. They would, however, be in for quite a shock as they'd have no choice but to play catch-up for many generations, if not longer, both culturally and technologically.

At the cargo bay entrance, a distinct odor entered

her nostrils. It was the same smell she'd noticed on her visit a day earlier, when she'd handed Jason Cassidy her résumé. She didn't know whether it was coming from the humans themselves or their ship. Regardless, whatever it was, she had no choice but to put up with it.

"Mirin!"

She peered across the cargo bay at the elevator car arriving on the lower deck. The man, who insisted he call her Jason, hopped out and made his way toward her with a large smile. He put out his hand, and she stared down at it curiously.

"Sorry," he said, retracting it. "It's an Earth custom that hasn't taken off out here yet."

Even though she found it slightly peculiar, she put out her own hand, and he shook it. "An odd custom indeed."

Jason laughed and gestured at their surroundings. "Welcome aboard the *Argo*. We might as well get started with your tour. This is C Deck, or the cargo bay. It's a pretty basic layout, but you'll find there's a lot of room down here considering the size of the ship." He led her toward the elevator, and they shot to the top of the shaft. "This is A Deck."

He allowed her to step out before him, and another waft, different to the first, smacked her in the face all at once. It was a rich blend of something she couldn't put her finger on. Strangely enough, it was quite pleasant.

Jason invited her to the bow of the deck and through a hatchway. "This is our bridge."

The interior of the small ship, though old, had a very warm feel about it. It exacerbated the age of the vessel due to the worn-in upholstery and patchwork quilt of paneling on the bulkheads.

"Like the cargo bay, it's pretty basic. We control systems and operations from opposite sides of the bridge, but when we need to, we can alter the settings and controls. Believe it or not, when this was built, it was actually ahead of its time, even compared to the ships of the CDF." Jason stopped by the chair in the center of the bridge. "You probably won't spend a great deal of time in here, but when you do, you'll be able to access our communications through the operations station."

"Thank you," she said.

They pressed on into the A Deck corridor. "Here we have the rec room," he told her, pointing inside it.

"Rec room?" Mirin stared in the unusually named compartment.

"It's where we come for recreation. When I was a kid growing up on this ship, we had a lot of free time between stops, especially with the old FTL drive we used to rock out on this thing. This place came in handy for all of us. It still does. We have a space to play cards, a ping-pong table, a chess set, and the sofas are still quite comfortable after all these years."

"An intriguing concept."

"Don't worry, you'll get the hang of this ship pretty quickly." Jason moved to the other side of the corridor. "In here's our galley."

The aroma she'd first smelled when arriving on A

Deck wafted its way through the door. At the table in the center of the kitchen facilities was one of the humans she'd met the day before.

"You remember Kevin?" Jason said.

She nodded and glanced at the ceramic mug in his hand. "Yes, of course."

The older man stood. "Welcome aboard, Mirin."

"Thank you."

"Kevin's our resident helmsman and healer of cuts and bruises when the need arises."

Mirin went closer and pointed at the beverage spewing steam from its top. "What is that?"

Kevin looked at his mug, and an amused smile curled from the edge of his mouth. "This is coffee."

"Coffee?"

"Would you like to try some?"

"Okay."

Kevin winked at Jason, and he trudged over to the other side of the galley and poured more of the brown substance. He returned with a mug of her own. "Be careful. It's hot."

He passed it to her, and she breathed in the aroma. Mirin took a sip, and the two humans watched her expectantly. She then guzzled the entire concoction, and their mouths dropped open.

"Are you okay?" Jason asked. "That was piping hot."

"My species are quite tolerant of boiling beverages," she informed him. "Back home we have similar drinks. Though I've never had something like this before."

"What do you think?" Kevin asked as she placed the mug back in his hand.

"It was...very nice."

"Well, there's plenty more where that came from. Believe me."

"Come on, let's keep moving." Jason gestured toward the door, and they went back to the corridor. He led her to the stern where they entered another compartment.

The cramped space shared many of the features of the rest of the ship, with the same weathered bulkheads, consoles, and worn deck plating. The lubricants of the old-style machinery whiffed through the air, filtering out the delightful smell from the galley.

Aly, the human female she'd met the day before at her interview, was hunched over a cubical device. She noticed them enter and turned. "Ah, our new arrival. Welcome to the engine room."

Mirin gazed around the beating heart of the *Argo*. "This ship obviously keeps you busy."

Aly's jovial nature faded but quickly returned. "You don't know the half of it. I hope Jason's been showing you all the ship's redeeming features. And don't let him tell you there aren't any. The *Argo* might be getting on in years, but she's still a reliable old girl."

Mirin shook her head in horror. "I assure you, he's—"

"Don't worry." Aly chuckled. "I was only kidding. A terrible joke."

Mirin darted her eyes between the two humans, suspecting, as she had the day before, that they were in some kind of bonding period. They may even be lifemates. Not wanting to pry, she returned her attention to whatever Aly was repairing. "What are you working on?

"This?" Aly placed her hands on her hips. "It's the engine from one of the hover lifters that injured a member of our crew."

"What's wrong with it?"

"Most of its old tech, so over time the components have degraded. It's at the point now that it might be easier just getting a new one."

Mirin took a step closer. "May I?"

"Of course."

Mirin placed her bags on the nearest console and kneeled, putting a hand inside the old-style machine. She examined the insides and grabbed at a conical-shaped component. "I assume this is the battery mechanism?"

The *Argo's* engineer joined her on the deck and nodded. "Yes."

"You're right. The internal workings of this engine have decayed greatly. However, there is a way to repair it so that it works like new."

"There is?"

Mirin jumped up and opened one of her bags, rummaging through it until she found the component she was after. She took the spherical-shaped device out and activated it.

Aly stared at the neon-blue glow emanating from its outer shell. "What is that?"

"A self-regenerating power pack." Mirin kneeled by the engineer's side on the deck again. "For a machine as basic as this hover lifter, it's effectively an infinite power source. You won't need to replace it for three hundred years."

"Three hundred years!"

Mirin pulled the old conical-shaped device from it and replaced it with the new one. Small tendrils peeled away from the powerpack and inserted themselves into the surrounding technology. "Not only will it give the lifter several lifetimes of power, but it'll regenerate the rest of the mechanisms inside it. You should never have to do maintenance on it ever again. Well, perhaps not until your great-great-great grandchildren have to replace it."

"Amazing." Aly took her handheld scanner from her belt and waved it over the engine. "Thank you. How can we repay you—"

Mirin waved her off. "I'm glad to help."

Jason assisted her up, and she grabbed her bags from the console. "Let's get you settled in, shall we?"

They left the engine room and went back to the elevator to take another ride. They finished up on B Deck, where the vile odor from earlier permeated more than anywhere else she'd visited.

"All our quarters and bathroom facilities are located here." Jason invited her out of the elevator, and she took a wary step out, doing her best not to show her discomfort. "I've organized your own quarters and—"

He stopped as someone emerged from the bathroom facilities at the far end of the deck. It was the only crewmember Mirin wasn't familiar with. The human male, similar in age to Kevin Rycroft, if not a little older, hobbled toward them on a set of crutches.

"Ah, Althaus," Jason said. "This is—"

The man walked by and ignored them with a scowl, rivaling any Mirin had ever seen.

"I apologize. With his injury, he's been a bit grumpy. Actually, that's not true. He's always a bit grumpy. But once you get to know him, you'll find he's a pretty good guy. Well, that's not overly true either..." Jason drifted off and changed the subject, moving toward the port side. "These will be your quarters. You're welcome to do with the décor what you wish. It's rather bland, so just go for it."

She opened the door to the room to discover how sparse the layout was. Apart from a bed and a closet, there wasn't much to work with. "Thank you, Jason."

"We'll be having lunch soon, so head up to the galley once you're settled in. If you need anything, just ask and I'll take care of it."

Mirin smiled warmly, and he left her on her own to enter her new lodging. She closed the door behind her and threw her bags on the bed. With a quick stroll around the small confines, she found the vents in the ceiling connected to the ship's climate-control system. She wondered how easy it would be to alter them to filter out the smell. Figuring it was a job for another day, she reached for one of her bags and grabbed her communicator.

She pressed it in, and a voice filtered from across the other end of the transmission. *"Yes, Mirin?"*

"I thought you'd like to know, I'm aboard," she said. "Everything is going just as we planned."

EIGHT

Brielaro

The tidally locked planet of the Kappa-Magellan star system filled the viewport at the front of the bridge as the Company ship pulled out of trans-space.

Javier, who hadn't taken his hands from the handrail since being called to the bridge, turned his head toward Onlor at the helm while he coordinated the ship's orbital insertion. With a direct instruction into his officer's ear, the *Brielaro* maneuvered to starboard and moved away from the light of the sun. Even the brightly lit bridge dimmed from the lack of natural illumination radiating from the heart of the star system.

Apart from some officers acknowledging an order from their superior, everyone remained deathly quiet while the vessel continued to round the eerily dead mass toward its darkest side. When everything went dark, that's when Javier spotted it. From its exterior it was a huge black jumble of twisted shapes, which somehow formed a circular profile. It was straight out of a nightmare. One that couldn't be forgotten.

"Professor?"

Javier turned again, to find Onlor staring at him from the rear of the platform near the scanners.

"Can you come over here?" he asked.

Javier wrenched his grasp from the handrail and headed over to the largest holographic console on the bridge. On it were meticulous readings of the station, much more detailed than anything he'd ever worked with.

The Ulvekan gestured toward the representation of the base with more scans rolling in. "I just want to confirm with you—"

"There's nothing to confirm," Javier told him. "This is definitely the Kalceni facility." He examined the scans closely. "One hundred and fifty kilometers in diameter, made of the same alloys as their vessels and the weapon ship. The only difference compared to the last time I was here, is that the facility appears completely inoperable and there are no ships."

"So, no one's home. Just as we suspected." Onlor grabbed the hologram and spun it around, finding an airlock for them to board. "Let's do what we came here to do."

The Company's main man led the way from the ship's command center. Javier eventually caught up with him after getting his weary bones moving. He realized he was nowhere near as quick as he used to be, but there was more stopping him from being so eager to return to the Kalceni base.

Some memories just can't be forgotten.

Both he and Onlor, along with a team of Company scientists and soldiers, boarded a transport vessel and departed the much larger *Brielaro*, making their way to one of the many airlocks left free by the Kalceni ships. Javier could still see the memory in his mind of the dark vessels maneuvering away from the vast station, opening a trans-space vortex and setting course for the heart of the Alliance. He thought the haunting images would have subsided after so long, but they were just as vivid as they'd ever been.

The helmsman gave Onlor the all clear and punched in a sequence of keys on his console to open the airlock, revealing the inner workings of the unforgettable Kalceni facility.

Onlor found Javier in the crowd of scientists and invited him forward. "It would only be appropriate that you lead the way, Professor."

Though he didn't see the point of such fanfare, he stepped toward the airlock regardless, with a team of armed Company soldiers. Both he and Onlor walked over the threshold together and entered the dark corridors, which matched the base's exterior tone.

"Which direction to the chamber?" the Ulvekan asked him.

Javier stopped in the middle of the corridor. The

rest of the expedition joined them and stared at him expectantly. For a moment he wondered what chamber Onlor was referring to. But there could only be one. He motioned forward, and the team continued on through the eerie confines until they reached an archway, confirming they were at their destination.

Onlor suddenly took the lead before Javier had a chance. Javier followed with the Company soldiers next to him, and the huge circular expanse hundreds of decks high appeared on the other side. And wrapping around the bulkheads were the individual hibernation pods, which were once filled with the many species the Kalceni had kidnapped to use as hosts.

The leader of the expedition remained a step ahead of the group and entered the solitary elevator. Javier entered, too, and the car moved up the shaft, coming to a halt at the top, exactly as it had the last time he'd visited. More empty hibernation pods greeted them, along with the most unique object on the entire base.

"The nexus..." Onlor whispered.

The octahedron-shaped object sat at the center of the circular upper level and was as big as a small craft. But unlike Javier's previous visit, it was drained of the life force which represented the Kalceni race. He pulled out his handheld scanner and confirmed it. What remained had been transferred into the host bodies, which went on to become the crew of the fleet that attacked the Alliance. And they were, of course, just as dead as the weapon ship they escorted.

Onlor stood before the nexus, almost hypnotized by the object. "It's phenomenal, isn't it?"

Javier nodded. "That's one way of describing it, I suppose."

Onlor pointed beyond another archway and set off again, farther into the Kalceni facility. It was extensive but nowhere near as sizeable as the huge hibernation chamber. Javier, with his scanner still in hand, took more readings of the area, which appeared somewhat similar to the combat control section of the Kalceni weapon ship they'd boarded at Psi-Aion. There was no focal point, but it was circular in shape and filled with banks of computers.

"What I wouldn't give for Kione to be here right now," he muttered.

"Did you say something, Professor?" Onlor asked.

"Don't mind me." Javier shook his head. "Just thinking about days gone by."

"What do you make of this?"

Javier walked over to the closest workstation he could find and ran his hands over the inoperable console. It was indeed similar in style to the computers on the weapon ship. "I'd surmise we're looking at the control point to every system on this base."

"Can you access it?"

"We'll need to start channeling power through this section. I think we can, but it will take some time."

"That's why I brought you along, Professor." Onlor glanced behind him as the rest of the expedition's science team arrived. "Use whatever resources we have at hand."

Javier nodded and examined the smooth obsidian controls. He could almost see the ghosts of the past lurking inside it.

NINE

Cargo Ship Argo

Jason stopped by the helm and inspected the auto-nav on the monitor at the heart of the console. As expected, the ship was holding steady inside the trans-space corridor for its journey to Vantar. The old girl was doing a commendable job. It had been especially tough for the *Argo* in the past few years. She hadn't been built for the several beatings she'd taken.

Jason leaned against the station and thought back to the simpler days of his childhood, when it would take months to get to their destination.

Decisions never had to be made at light speed.

He had one more look through the viewport at the swirling colors enveloping them and walked out into the corridor toward the elevator. He directed it to C Deck, and it shuddered to life, taking him down to the lowest level of the small ship. He stepped into the cargo bay where the extent of their shipment bound for Vantar appeared before him. Every corner of the bay was chock-full.

They'd initially only signed on to deliver one hundred and twenty containers, but Mirin had somehow bent the laws of physics, and their buyer agreed to take on more if they could ship it. Jason naturally said yes.

He strode toward her at the center of the bay, to find the newest addition of his crew looking over a data tablet. "This is fantastic work."

She glanced up. "Thank you."

"One has to ask how you managed to pack so much in down here."

"With the extra support bracing for the containers on top, we should have no problem maximizing the space in here by another fifteen percent in the future."

"Along with fifteen percent extra profits."

"Exactly."

Jason spotted Althaus stumbling around on his crutches, checking out the cargo with a data tablet of his own. He'd completely ignored Kevin's instructions to take it easy and decided to help Mirin instead. "She's going to put you out of a job, Uncle!"

Althaus merely scowled at him and returned to his work.

"How's he been?" Jason asked her

"Fine."

"You'll probably find his bark's bigger than his bite."

She raised her eyes at the remark. "An interesting way of putting it, but I suppose it's accurate. In truth, I quite like him. You always know what you're going to get with him."

"That's for sure." Jason marched toward one of the containers and inspected the bracing they'd acquired at Mirin's recommendation. "I actually came down here to invite you to our poker night."

"Poker." She put her tablet by her side and craned her neck.

"Yeah, it's a type of card game." He walked back to her. "Remember, recreation? It helps blow off steam. It's also fun to win some money off each other."

"Ah." She nodded. "You're talking about gambling."

"Well, I guess, yeah. We don't play with a lot of money, though."

"I've come across my fair share of gambling games on my other jobs over the years."

"Does that mean you'll join us?"

"Sure. I might just watch a bit before playing, though. I don't want to lose all my earnings straight away on a new game."

"Excellent." Jason smiled. "I'll see you in the rec room at twenty hundred hours."

"This is brutal."

Jason threw his cards down, revealing his miserly two pair against Mirin's full house on the opposite side of the table. He stared ominously at the large stack of chips in the pot.

"Does that mean I've won?" Mirin asked.

Aly pushed the chips toward Mirin, adding to her already burgeoning collection. "They're all yours."

"Brutal isn't the word I'd use to describe this," Kevin said to his right. "I'm thinking more like—"

"Hilarious?" Aly chimed in.

"Yes. Hilarious. That's exactly what this is."

Jason glared at the two Rycrofts on either side of him while the ship's newbie piled her winnings high in front of her.

After twenty minutes of watching the trio go about the game of Cerberan Poker, she'd jumped in and immediately started winning.

"Neither of you are faring much better," Jason retorted, indicating their tiny stacks.

"Yes, but we have an excuse. We've never been that good," Kevin said. "You, well... It would appear we have a new champion in town."

Aly chuckled. "It's so good to have another girl on the *Argo* to shore up the numbers."

Jason shook his head, doing everything in his power not to laugh at the jokes being pulled at his expense. Mirin stayed out of the gentle ribbing, concentrating on counting her chips.

"I have to admit, it is nice to have someone else around here," he said. "To think, when we left for the Reach, we had Doctor Tai, Marissa, and Kione all aboard with us."

The woman's ears pricked up. "Kione?"

"Yes, he—"

"Don't worry, I know who Kione is." She placed her hands on either side of her winnings. "Or at least the myth that is Kione."

"Myth?"

"The destroyer of the Kalceni."

"Well, I guess that's one way of describing him."

"So, it's true then?" she asked. "He did exist?"

Jason chortled, remembering his friend. An image flashed in his mind of the first time they'd met on Orion V. "Kione is...was indeed real."

"Everything about your journey and how you defeated the Kalceni almost sounds fantastical." Mirin leaned forward. "Can I ask what he was like?"

Jason fiddled with his chips and looked down at the table. "He was a good man."

"I bet you miss him."

He stared past her at the trans-space corridor beyond the viewport. "Like you wouldn't believe."

"Well, I suppose there can be no greater sacrifice than saving the galaxy."

"Bridge to rec room."

Jason snapped out of his daydream, remembering his friend, and activated his commband. "Go ahead."

"You might want to get up here," Althaus said.

Everyone at the poker table shared an uneasy glace and dashed from their seats, rushing up the corridor to the bridge.

"What have you got?" Jason asked Althaus who was stooped beside the operations console.

"A distress call." He pressed at the comm to play the message.

"This is Commander Korval of the freighter Mortsrem. *We are under attack. I repeat, we are under attack. Please, anyone that receives this, help us, we—"*

The transmission ceased and was replaced with white noise.

"Where's it coming from?" Aly asked.

Althaus reached over and winced, activating the scanners. "We're due in the next ten minutes to come out of this gateway and transit to another in the next star system over. It appears to be emanating between the two."

Jason rubbed his chin. "Get the exact coordinates and send them to the helm. Kevin, once we're clear of the gateway, set a course."

TEN

The *Argo* closed in on the coordinates of the distress call, and the freighter appeared at the heart of the bridge's viewport. The vessel was at least ten times the size of their own quaint little cargo ship, and its hull painted light gray, making it appear as if it were a beached whale in the night.

"Well, it's still intact," Jason said, approaching Kevin at the helm.

"Barely," Aly informed them from the operations station. "It's been severely damaged. I'm detecting debris from the starboard section. From what I can tell, four decks have been breached."

"Do you recognize it?" Jason asked Mirin.

Their new crewmember stepped forward from the rear of the bridge. "That's a Trevien merchant vessel."

Kevin punched the *Argo's* maneuvering thrusters, and the ship circled to the opposite side of the freighter to make a visual inspection of the tears in the hull.

"I'm reading energy weapon discharges," Aly said. "There's no doubt about it, she was definitely attacked."

Jason scratched his head. "Could this be the result of piracy? It is a freighter after all."

Mirin shook her head. "Piracy doesn't exist in the Alliance."

While Jason would have once been shocked at such a statement, he'd been in Alliance space for long enough to know she was telling the truth. "Aly, can you detect any other ships in the area? Perhaps their assailant?"

She shook her head. "The board's clear."

"Open a commlink."

"Commlink open."

"Freighter *Mortsrem*, this is Jason Cassidy of the *Cargo Ship Argo*, answering your distress call. Please respond."

White noise filtered over the speakers.

"Captain Korval, come in," he repeated.

Silence again answered.

"Close the commlink." Jason paced in front of the captain's chair. "Seems as if we'll have to go over there and take a look for ourselves. Aly, get your tools."

At the operations station, Althaus struggled to move from his seat, nearly stumbling over onto his face.

"And where do you think you're going?" Jason glared at him. "Sit your ass back down." He sidled up to Mirin at the front of the bridge. "Fancy coming along?"

She raised her eyebrows.

Freighter Mortsrem

Jason took the first step through the airlock from the *Julieanne*, and his two female crew members took up the rear. As a precautionary measure they wore their EV suits and were all armed. Not a single flash of illumination beamed through from anywhere, creating an eerily dark welcome. He turned on the flashlight on the arm of his suit, and the pair followed his lead.

Aly pointed her handheld scanner into the blackness before them. "I'm afraid to say we'll have to keep our suits on. It seems there are more breaches here than I thought."

"Damn." Jason hated the suits with a passion, but he enjoyed asphyxiating even less. He continued down the corridor until they found themselves at an intersection. "Do you know your way around one of these ships?" he asked Mirin.

She stopped beside him and beamed her flashlight down the many avenues. "I've never worked aboard this class of freighter before, but I visited a similar Trevien vessel several years ago."

"Any idea where they'd store their cargo?"

Mirin pointed to their left. "Usually to the stern and down."

Jason took the lead, this time with Mirin by his side, and his rifle aiming to the fore. Aly trailed behind them with her scanner in one hand and a sidearm in the other. They eventually hit the end of a corridor and tried their luck at the elevator nearby. But it didn't work. Mirin found an emergency ladder chute, and they climbed down the rungs all the way to the lowest level.

"You were right on the money." Jason gazed at the enormous four doors on either side of him. He walked to one of them and attempted to access the terminal next to it, randomly mashing the keypad.

Obviously noticing his lack of luck, Mirin came up beside him and made another attempt. The gigantic door in front of them clanged open and revealed a massive hold, at least five times bigger than the cargo bay on the *Argo*. She went to the other three doors and opened them in sequence, revealing similar sections all filled to the brim with cargo.

"You're right, there is no piracy in the Alliance, is there?" Jason quipped at the motherlode they'd stumbled upon. "The question is, why were the Treviens attacked?"

The team pressed on until they reached the engine room. All three went their separate ways to see if they could find any of the crew, or some clue as to their demise. Jason searched up and down the vast space with no luck and stopped at the central section in the middle of a bank of computers.

Aly appeared a moment later. "I'm guessing you didn't turn up anything."

"No, nothing. And no one." Jason scratched his head. "What the hell happened here? If no one's stealing their cargo, what are they doing attacking a merchant ship? This is the Alliance. It's not as if we're in some backwater."

"Like the commonwealth?"

Jason chuckled at the disparaging remarks aimed at their home. His smile quickly faded, and Mirin appeared from around the corner of the large trans-space engine. "How did you go?" he asked her.

"None of the ship's tech has been stolen if that's what you're referring to," she said.

"It just doesn't make sense..."

"Perhaps we should go to the bridge," Aly suggested.

"Good idea." Jason gestured to the exit, and the trio moved farther up the vessel, finding another ladder chute which took them to one of the upper decks. With their destination in reach, he put up his hand on the last rung. "What the hell?"

He pulled his hand away to find it covered in a red tacky substance. Without saying a word to the others, he made the jump onto the deck above.

A river of blood greeted him, and collapsed throughout it were the slaughtered bodies of the *Mortsrem's* crew. "Dear God..."

Aly gasped as she emerged from the chute, while Mirin's eyes widened at the discovery.

Jason walked toward one of the slain bodies and kicked a rifle out of their hands. "Whoever attacked the ship obviously boarded." He kneeled beside the downed Trevien, conscious not to get any blood on his pants. "Energy weapon wounds and lacerations."

The trio tiptoed through the gauntlet of death all the way to the end of the corridor, where an archway welcomed them to the bridge of the ship. Though smaller than other sections of the freighter, the beating heart of it was much larger than the *Argo* command center. Throughout were a smattering of bodies slumped over their chairs and sprawled over the deck. All were just as dead as their compatriots from outside the hatchway. But it was what was on the viewport which was that much more shocking.

Jason crept up to the blood spattered over it in odd patterns. "Are these words?"

While Aly pottered around the rest of the bridge, Mirin approached him, inspecting the horrific sight. "That's Quarlini."

"Quar-what?" Jason asked.

"Quarlini is the language of the Quarons."

"And who are they?"

"The Quarons and Treviens share neighboring star systems. Well before the Alliance ever made contact with their worlds, they thought they were the only inhabitants in the entire galaxy. Let's just say, neither got along too well. But when the Alliance eventually revealed themselves, they had no choice but to resolve their differences to join the intergalactic neighborhood."

"It would seem hostilities have resumed."

"A shot hasn't been fired in over three hundred years. War in the Alliance is not tolerated. It's been the fundamental building block of what the organization was founded on." Mirin stopped and looked away. "Though perhaps that's all changing."

"What do you mean?" Jason asked.

"Hmm? Oh, just rumors really." She sighed. "Apparently, this isn't the first time old rivalries have come to the fore since the Kalceni attack. Some believe it's tarnished the Alliance's invincibility, and their capacity to keep the peace after such a large part of their fleet was destroyed. If that's correct, what we've witnessed here is but the start of further destabilization."

Jason's mind flashed to when he was on Mascoros Prime and what the seemingly crazy Mascoron cleric had said to him.

"You have stepped from the light into the darkness. Much like the problems recently in your commonwealth, the Alliance, too, is facing a similar threat from the shadow of the Kalceni."

"The prophecies say that there are still battles to be fought. What we are witnessing here is but the beginning. Those who follow the old ways from the Retebu and the Kalceni are mobilizing. Our modern civilizations are but the battlegrounds for the ancient conflict."

Jason snapped back to reality. "Mirin, can you read what that says?"

She didn't say anything at first but eventually pointed at the symbols. "Your final hour is at hand. Darkness is coming."

"Argo to Jason," Kevin's voice resonated over his commband.

Jason stared at Mirin at the revelation and slowly brought his commband to his face. "Go ahead."

"We've got a bogey on an intercept course."

"The Quarons..."

Mirin nodded.

"I think it's time we got back to the ship." He turned to Aly who was arm deep in a maintenance junction at the rear of the bridge. "Gather your things. We're getting the hell out of here."

ELEVEN

Cargo Ship Argo

Jason marched onto the bridge with Aly and Mirin close behind him. While they'd left their helmets back on the *Julieanne,* they hadn't had time to remove the rest of their EV suits, much to his chagrin.

"All right, what are we looking at here?" he asked Althaus.

"Well, we're not dealing with another freighter," he said.

Jason invited Mirin to follow him, and the pair peered over his uncle's shoulder at the scanners. "Do you recognize it?"

She sighed. "It's a Quaron warship."

"Makes the most sense." Althaus bought up detailed scans of the incoming bogey. "It's armed to the teeth."

Jason gazed across at Kevin. "How long will it take to get to the gateway?"

"Not even a second at FTL, but the calculations would have to be precise," his helmsman said.

"I gather you've already done them."

"Of course."

"Prepare to go to FTL."

"Wait!" Aly yelled.

Everyone turned to her, and Jason hurried over to the operations station. "What is it?"

"We can't fire up our FTL engines."

"Why not?"

"Because this entire area of space has been saturated in Iota particles."

"From the Trevien ship?"

Aly nodded. "The attack by the Quarons must have damaged their engine bay so badly the particles leaked out into open space."

"And if we got to FTL—"

"We can't. Our plasma exhausts are likely full of the particles as we speak."

"Does that mean boom?"

Aly nodded again. "That means boom."

Jason frowned. "Kevin, best speed at sub-light. Now."

"On our way," he replied, blasting the *Argo* in the opposite direction to the incoming bogey.

Jason rested his hand on the back of Aly's chair. "Open a commlink. Let's see if we can let these guys know we mean them no harm."

She tapped at her console. "Commlink open."

"Quaron vessel, this is Jason Cassidy of the *Cargo Ship Argo*. I—"

"Cargo Ship Argo," the guttural accent boomed over the speakers from the opposing vessel. *"You have entered Quaron territory. We demand to know why you've crossed into our space."*

"Aly, mute commlink." Jason furrowed his brow. "Bring up a star chart of the region. Mirin, could you come here?"

Their new crewmember joined them at the operations station.

"Where are we with regard to the Quaron and Trevien home worlds?" he asked her.

Mirin pointed to the pair of major stars on the graphic. "If your scanners are accurate, we're somewhere between the two systems, though I suppose technically a little closer to Quaron Prime. But since there are no borders—"

"But before the Alliance there was a border, wasn't there?"

"Well, yes. A hotly contested one. And I'd imagine this particular region was once Quaron space."

Jason recalled the blood streaming down the deck of the Trevien freighter. "Reopen the commlink, Aly."

She nodded, signifying he was back on.

"Quaron warship," he continued, "we are not aware of such borders. As far as we understand we are in Alliance space and are permitted here under the Alliance Merchant Act which gives us free rein throughout—"

"The Quaron Directorate no longer recognizes those boundaries."

"What do you mean you no longer recognize these boundaries?"

"You are to explain why you are in Quaron territory and why you boarded an enemy vessel of the Directorate."

Jason touched Aly's shoulder again, and she muted the channel. "Mirin, what's going on here? Could we be dealing with a radical Quaron element?"

The alien woman bit her lower lip. "The Directorate's the ruling body over all internal Quaron affairs. If they are legitimate, they wholeheartedly believe we've veered into their territory."

He nodded at Aly, and she reopened the commlink. "Quaron warship, it would appear there's been some kind of mistake. Our star charts have not been updated since the change in border markings. On our journey through a trans-space corridor, we detected a distress call we thought was coming from inside Alliance space. We apologize for the misunderstanding and ask if you'll allow us to leave your territory in peace."

Jason felt horrible taking such a cowardly way out. Especially after what he'd seen on the freighter. But their crew was dead and his weren't. He had to ensure they didn't perish like the Treviens.

"Cargo Ship Argo, *you are to bring your engines to a full stop and prepare to be boarded. Your crew will be charged for trespassing by the Quaron Directorate and your ship impounded."*

Jason checked the scanners, hoping to see another bogey. Another Trevien vessel. An Alliance patrol ship. Anything. But the board was clear. "Quaron warship, I again apologize for the inconvenience, but I cannot allow that. We have an urgent consignment to deliver and will incur a heavy fee if we don't reach our destination on time. Being impounded and imprisoned won't make my employers very happy."

He squeezed Aly's shoulder, and she muted the frequency again. "Kevin, how far away from the gateway are we?"

He swiveled around from the helm. "With the pace they're gaining? Too far."

"I was afraid you'd say that." Jason turned to his uncle. "Althaus, let's activate those shields we recently acquired. Time to give them a proper shakedown."

Althaus nodded, and on the operations station a graphic appeared of the shields firing up and bathing a halo of energy around the *Argo*.

"They're getting a little impatient," Aly said, indicating the muted commlink.

"Put them back on," Jason instructed her.

"Cargo Ship Argo, *if you do not comply with our instructions, we'll have no other option but to open fire,*" the Quaron captain demanded from the pursuing warship.

"Surely we can come to some kind of arrangement." Jason paced back to the middle of the bridge. "We have a—"

"They've terminated the commlink." Aly glanced over at him.

"And we were getting along so well."

"Hold on to your hats, everyone," she said. "They're preparing to fire!"

TWELVE

The bridge quaked around Jason and the rest of the crew as the Quaron warship fired potshots at the much smaller cargo vessel. Like every alien ship they'd come across since journeying beyond the Reach, it used an array of energy weapons to project its power. The most advanced CDF cruiser would be outmatched with a full arsenal at its disposal, let alone the *Argo*.

Kevin wrestled with the helm, performing every kind of evasive maneuver in the book, along with a few that didn't exist. The man who'd taught Jason from the moment he could reach the *Argo's* controls, managed to weave the ship away from many of their pursuer's shots, but even he couldn't stop all the hits from striking their stern.

"Probably wasn't a bad idea picking up that shield system after all." Jason shared a knowing glance with his uncle. "How are they holding up?"

The *Argo* again took another hit on the rear shield. Even though it was doing its job ensuring the hull remained intact along with their lives, it still shuddered Jason to his core.

"Just enough for now, but they won't last forever," Althaus said. "Every hit we take drains them further. Before long we'll be as naked as the day you were born."

Jason checked the scanners on his command console to find they were still too far from the gateway. He had hoped his wits would have come up with a means to save them by now, but even he was beginning to think he was finally out of ideas. He was about to ask for suggestions, but Mirin unbuckled herself from the emergency seats at the rear of the bridge and approached him.

"We need to go back to the Trevien freighter," she said in her typically calm demeanor.

"The Trevien freighter?" Jason glowered. "Are you kidding me?"

Both Althaus and Aly looked at the pair at the center of the bridge. No doubt Kevin would have done the same if he wasn't riding the helm like a cowboy.

"I don't think you understand the predicament we're in," Jason said.

"I understand completely the predicament we're in."

Jason thought back to a few days earlier when she'd wrestled the huge green goon in the bar, not only saving his life and Aly's, but doing it in style. There was something about the woman he hadn't quite been able to put his finger on. She was confident, forthright, and very aware of what was going on around her. He hurried down to Kevin, whose hands were frantically dashing across his console. "We have to turn back."

"That'll be very difficult," he told him, keeping his eyes on his controls. "If we attempt a loop to starboard or port, we'll be giving them a much larger target to hit. Even you'd struggle to stop us from being blown to pieces."

"Flattering as always." Jason leaned over and thumbed at the keypad. "What if we went straight at them?"

"I—"

"Think about it. They won't see it coming. Their weapon emitters are on the dorsal hull of their ship. Sure, we'll take a few hits, but when we're too close they won't be able to get a lock and we can ride under them and back toward the Trevien freighter." He turned to Althaus. "These shields can be adapted, right?"

Althaus nodded. "If you're asking if I can route all the energy to the bow, then yes."

"Good. Get ready to distribute the power."

Kevin appeared to do some internal arithmetic in his head, all the while dodging another blast. "I suppose it's possible, but Althaus will have to ensure he doesn't alter the shields' setting until I've brought the *Argo* about."

"You just concentrate on flying, Rycroft. I'll take care of the rest," Althaus told him.

Jason smirked and patted Kevin on the shoulder, returning to the captain's chair. "Okay, let's do it!"

Kevin maneuvered the old girl down the z-axis as fast as she could go and returned on an identical path to which they'd come. The viewport filled with the beast that was the Quaron warship. It was even more menacing than when they'd first made contact. He kept the *Argo* low, and for a moment they avoided the weapon fire, still aiming at their previous position. But it didn't take them long to figure out what was going on, and they retrained their target on their new course. Kevin did everything he could to evade the fire, but there were only so many maneuvers he could pull out.

The Quarons hit them hard, forcing Mirin to buckle herself back in at the rear of the bridge. The deck shuddered, and the hull groaned, while the lights flickered around them.

"Shields are nearly depleted!" Althaus yelled over the din of the Quaron firepower.

Jason grasped hold of his seat, riding every blow coming the *Argo's* way.

Then silence filled the bridge, and the shaking stopped.

Through the viewport, the ventral hull of the attacking ship appeared, and the weapon fire came to a halt. The *Argo* pushed on and flew past the warship's stern and beyond it toward the Trevien freighter.

"The Quarons are turning," Aly informed him from her scanners.

Mirin unstrapped herself again and returned to the center of the bridge. "Will we reach the freighter before they get to us?"

"Only just," Aly replied.

"What's your plan, Mirin?" Jason asked.

She passed by him without answering and stood next to Kevin. "May I?"

Jason hopped out of the captain's chair and took up a position on the opposite side of the helm. "Okay."

"Once we reach the freighter, I want you to stop above its dorsal hull," she directed Kevin.

The helmsman glanced at Jason. "Are you sure about this?"

Jason wished he had an answer to the question. "Just do it."

The *Argo* continued to bound toward the freighter and quickly closed on the larger vessel.

Jason eyed Aly on the starboard side of the bridge at her station. He wanted to desperately say something to her, fearing he might not have another chance. "How far behind us are they?"

"Twelve seconds," Kevin said.

"Mirin, I really need to know what you're doing. In under twelve seconds—"

"Jason, please, I'm concentrating." She pulled out a handheld device from her pocket and activated it, lighting up a tiny red display.

"What is that?" he asked.

"Shh!"

"Coming up on the freighter now," Kevin told them.

"Bring us to a stop," Mirin said.

Kevin did as he was instructed and put on the brakes. The *Argo* slowed rapidly, using its forward thrusters to halt their momentum.

Then everyone waited.

They all darted their eyes at Mirin as she pressed the keypad on her device. It flashed green, and a series of alien numbers or letters scrolled down the tiny screen.

She checked the scanners and put her hand on Kevin's shoulder. "When I give you the word, I want you to move us out of here as fast as you can."

He nodded, and the Quaron warship closed, almost stopping right on top of them.

"I'm reading an energy buildup in their weapon emitters!" Aly yelled.

"Althaus, whatever's left in those shields, reroute all power to the stern," Jason said.

"Go now!" Mirin commanded.

Kevin punched the main thrusters, and Mirin pressed the button on the middle of her device. The next thing Jason knew, a bright white light surrounded him and the rest of the bridge.

THIRTEEN

Mirin wondered what hit her. It certainly wasn't the big green Tiruglien from the bar on Myjurna Station.

As she opened her eyes and adjusted to the light, she took in the cramped confines with two other beds and cabinets full of medical equipment. The soft beep of a computer filled her ears, in a hypnotizing beat which matched her own heart rate. She dragged herself up, but a spell of dizziness threw her back against the pillow.

"It looks like someone's awake."

She tilted her head sideways to find someone walking toward her. She attempted to lift herself again, but the man's warm hands ensured she remained still.

"Please, you're better just resting for now," he said.

"Kevin?" She finally recognized the man. "I'm on the *Argo*?"

"Very good." His mouth turned up at the edges. "It appears that bang to the head hasn't done much damage after all."

She touched her forehead to find some bandages wrapped around it. "The Quarons..."

Kevin stepped away from her bed and thumbed a panel next to one of the medical cabinets. "Kevin to Jason. Mirin has regained consciousness back here."

"Thanks. I'll be right there," came the reply on the other end of the transmission.

Kevin walked back toward her and waved a medical scanner over her body. It beeped, much more violently than the monitor keeping check on her heart rate.

"What's my prognosis?" she asked.

Before he could say anything, another figure entered the cargo ship's infirmary and joined the older human on the other side of the bed.

The younger man peered down at her with pale features, but they immediately brightened at the sight of her. "How is she?"

"While I'm no expert on Mirin's physiology, the whack she took flying into that bulkhead on the bridge caused significant head trauma." Kevin showed Jason a series of the scans he'd taken and directed him to the monitor behind her bed. "If these were human readings, I'd say she was lucky to not be in a coma. But as we've seen on our travels, every species is different."

"I suppose the important thing is, how do you feel?" Jason asked her.

"Like I've been in a tournament against a prize fighter. And lost," she said, again dabbing at her wound.

Jason stared across at his elder. "What's your thoughts from here on out?"

"Considering I have no idea what I'm really looking at when it comes to her scans, I'd like to keep her in the infirmary for a while longer just to monitor her. If she improves, I can take an educated guess and say she's on the mend. With that said, once we reach Vantar, I think it'd be prudent to get her examined by a doctor who knows more about her physiology."

"We can arrange that."

"Vantar?" Mirin reached out with her hands, which seemed to blur in front of her. She clutched Jason by the arm and drew him closer. "Does that mean we got away from the Quarons?"

"Well, it seems you remember something." Jason grinned, and he pulled her handheld detonator from his pocket.

She yanked it from him and read through the data streaming down the screen. "It worked?"

"You could say that." Jason grabbed a chair from behind him and sat. "Once Kevin began hightailing it, you pressed that thing of yours and the Trevien freighter blew up into a giant fireball, badly damaging the Quaron vessel."

"It didn't destroy them?"

"Amazingly not. Whatever their ship is made of, it's certainly got a strong hide. Luckily they're in no condition to come after us anymore." He leaned forward. "What exactly did you do when we were over there?"

"Bought us insurance." She tapped her detonator. "Let's just say I wanted to guarantee our survival should something unexpected happen. I rigged the Trevien freighter's power core to blow in case we needed it."

Jason chuckled and shook his head. "You're full of surprises, Mirin."

"Is that a bad thing?" she asked.

"Not when it saves our lives. Thank you." He stood. "Now, rest up and do what Kevin tells you. Contrary to what he might say, he's actually pretty good at this stuff."

Mirin nodded, and at the hatchway, another visitor appeared.

"Jason," Aly said, peering in and smiling at her. "Can I see you?"

"Sure." Jason walked to the door and took one last look at Mirin before departing. She then closed her eyes and attempted to get comfortable, thinking about the mission at hand and what was yet to come.

Jason moved into the corridor with Aly. "What is it?"

She stopped by the elevator at the heart of A Deck. "I thought you'd like to know that I've purged the plasma exhausts of the errant Iota particles."

"Good work. What about the rest of the ship?"

"Luckily, our shields, even in their weakened state, took the brunt of the blast. However, that doesn't mean there's still not a lot to do."

"What about the FTL drive?"

"It's not in the space I'd like it, but I can give it to you for a limited time."

"Best news I've heard all day." Jason breathed a sigh of relief. "All we need to do is reach the gateway, then we can ride the trans-space corridor the rest of the way to Vantar."

"Can you come in here?"

They both turned toward his uncle, who was standing at the hatchway to the bridge, propping himself up with his crutches. Jason and Aly glanced at each other curiously and followed him onto the bridge, where Althaus directed them to the systems station.

"I'm detecting a series of bogeys coming out of the gateway we took to get here," he said. "They're heading toward the damaged Quaron vessel."

Jason examined the six vessels on the monitor. "They're not of Quaron design. Perhaps an Alliance patrol heard the Treviens' distress call, too."

"Maybe. Or it could be Quarons have allies."

"Perhaps. If what Mirin says is true, the political situation here is unpredictable at best."

"Which means we can't be certain if they're friend or foe," Aly said.

"Right. And I don't particularly want to find out." Jason rubbed his chin. "It might be time to fire up that FTL drive."

She nodded and hurried off to the helm.

Jason followed her and put a hand on the back of her seat. "Plot a course for the gateway and get us moving."

Aly plugged in the coordinates, while Jason spotted a large chunk of the upholstery peeled away from the seat.

"What if there's more of this to come?"

"Hmm?" he said to her, lost in thought.

"We've had it pretty good for a while out here." Aly sailed the *Argo* toward the gateway. "Do you think the rumors Mirin was saying are true?"

Jason recalled what the cleric on Mascoros Prime had told him. "She's been right about everything so far."

"Then what does that mean for us if the Alliance is unraveling around us?"

Jason poked at the chunk taken from the chair and threw it to the deck. "We'll be okay, Aly. We always are."

He thought more about what he'd seen on the Trevien vessel. The river of blood had created a tableau difficult to forget. Aly was right. Instability in the Alliance would be inconvenient for a crew who had gotten used to roaming the stars and making good money. For the galaxy as a whole, however, it would be disastrous.

FOURTEEN

Brielaro

Javier stood in front of the enormous table at the heart of the Company ship's laboratory, created specifically for their expedition. Dozens of different mechanisms and devices lay across it, while the scientists collected for the mission studied the individual pieces.

Some brought back from the Kalceni base were easily identified, but others were more obtuse and unlike anything Javier could conceive. It was a treasure trove that would likely keep the scientists of the Alliance occupied for years, if not decades to come.

Javier yawned after what had been a very long day working hard inside the enormous Kalceni base. He was glad to be back in a friendlier and much brighter environment aboard the *Brielaro*. Once upon a time he would have looked at the clock and waved it off, forgoing food to continue with his work. But more increasingly his body was telling him no more. He needed sustenance. And sleep.

Behind him, a holographic console beeped to life, and he turned to activate it. He did his best to access the interface, even though he was still a little uncertain about the alien technology. Thankfully, they'd adapted their computers to a familiar language for him, and in English, DOWNLOAD COMPLETE flashed in front of a plethora of data points. He pressed in the holographic controls, and a large chunk of data appeared. It, however, wasn't in English but Kalceni. Luckily for him, it was a language he'd become familiar with since his first visit to the Kappa-Magellan system.

Javier scrolled through what effectively amounted to computer code. Albeit much more advanced compared to anything he was used to back at home. But as with everything, there were always patterns. And he was a master at not only finding them but disseminating them. He wondered if he should get a bite to eat first, but the old Javier Petit raised its head and stopped him in his tracks.

He proceeded through the data until he found his way inside. A menu appeared, familiar to what he'd seen on the Kalceni weapon ship. Unfortunately, while on the base, they'd been unable to get the ship's hardware operating, but the software was a different story. Now it was just a matter of transferring it to the *Brielaro* and translating it line by line until he gained access.

An hour passed, and then two, before he finally handed out various sections of the code to his colleagues so they could attack it as a team. Then, just as he was about to take a break and relieve his rumbling stomach, something popped up on his interface, piquing his curiosity.

"Are those star charts?" Doctor Unaporvan asked at the terminal beside him.

"I believe so." Javier moved his hands through the air, sifting through the files, and checked each of them, discovering several different maps.

He put the Kalceni data to one side for a moment and linked them up with the star charts from the *Brielaro's* computer. The two pools of data then overlaid with one another, matching the stars from each. The *Brielaro's* database recognized most of them, but there were quite a few it didn't.

"They must be in the unexplored systems beyond the Alliance's borders," Unaporvan said.

Javier nodded and continued. A distinct pattern emerged regarding how the Kalceni named the star systems. "These are all numbers."

He then stopped at one map in particular.

Unaporvan leaned in toward the holographic projection. "What are you looking at there, Professor?"

Javier didn't say anything immediately, instead double-checking to make sure he'd found what he thought he had. "Somewhere where all roads lead. Onlor is going to be very interested in this."

"Aren't you already in his good books?" the doctor quipped. "Leave something for the rest of us to discover."

Javier was too tired to bite at the gentle ribbing, instead getting up from his seat and glancing at the time. Food and sleep would again have to wait.

Onlor hacked the same nasty dry cough he'd had for at least three years. It was always worse as the day went on. But thankfully, during the morning and afternoon, with the right medication, he was rid of the parched sensation which permeated down his throat. Night was the enemy, however, and whenever he tried to medicate, sleep would completely allude him.

He lay on the sofa in his office and rested his head on a small cushion. He should have gone to bed, but there was too much frustration bubbling inside him since returning from the Kalceni Base. He'd been fighting for so long to reach the Kappa-Magellan system, so he couldn't help but be disappointed when he was told the station was filled with inoperative technology, which the Kalceni likely sabotaged when they left.

Just as his eyelids wavered, his door chime sounded.

He growled under his breath and heaved himself up. "Open!"

The doors parted, and Onlor brushed the creases from his Company uniform. He shielded his eyes for a moment as a figure stepped through into the dimly lit room.

"I'm not disturbing you, am I?" his visitor asked,

stopping in front of the light to reveal himself as the solitary human on his expedition.

"Not at all, Professor," he said wearily to Petit, lightly coughing, doing his best to push it down. "Please come in."

The human entered, and the door closed behind him, bathing the office again in darkness.

"Fifty percent illumination." Onlor made his way to his desk and took a seat while the lights increased, but not so much that they hurt his eyes. He invited the professor to sit in front of his desk. "What can I do for you at this time of the evening?"

Petit fell into the chair and rubbed his eyelids, no doubt as equally fatigued as him. "I thought you'd like to know that I managed to access the Kalceni database today."

"That's something, I guess." Ever since reading up on the initial Earth expedition, Onlor knew he needed to have Javier Petit on his team. When he'd traveled to Earth to ask for his services, he wasn't going to take no for an answer. The professor was an absolute necessity for his mission. In the end, he didn't have to be too persuasive, and Petit came along regardless. "What have you found?"

The professor gestured to the computer on his desk.

"Please." Onlor waved at the holographic controls, and his late-night visitor activated them, bringing up a series of maps between the pair above his desk.

"I've discovered an array of star charts inside the computer, and I've matched them with the ones in your own database." He directed the holographic interface to label each star with a Kalceni symbol. "From what I can determine, the Kalceni don't name stars or planets but rather number them. Also, the larger the number, the more likely it is to be farther out from a central focal point."

"A central focal point?" Onlor scratched his chin. "Are you saying you've been able to track down the Kalceni home world?"

Petit brought up another image, this time with four stars on it. Each, like the others, had a Kalceni digit next to it. "I believe these are the Kalceni's core worlds. Or at least they were six million years ago prior to the great war with the Retebu."

"I assume I'm looking at star systems one through four."

Petit shook his head. "Zero to three, actually."

"Zero? Why zero?"

"I don't know. But regardless, I think Star System Zero could in fact be the home of the Kalceni."

Onlor leaned back and stared at the one particular point of light. "Where is it?"

Petit zoomed out, revealing a much broader picture of the region. "This is the area we on Earth call Frontier's Reach. Beyond its position farther toward the center of the galaxy is the location of Star System Zero. Far beyond the unexplored systems of the Alliance."

"How far are we talking?"

"It's obviously nowhere near the gateway network, but I've liaised with the bridge, and they claim we can be at the coordinates within the week using the Brielaro's trans-space engine."

Onlor did everything in his power to stop himself from coughing in front of the professor and sat tall. "What do you think we'll find out there?"

"Hard to say." Petit shrugged. "Everything we know points to the fact the Kalceni are extinct. The only remnants that we believe outlived the great war were those we found on that base out there. But I would guess, if there is anything left of them from six million years ago, it will be there. I naturally advise caution."

"Don't forget why we're out here." Onlor waved over the hologram, and an image of his helmsman appeared before him. "Bridge, I'm sending you some coordinates. Once our people are back from the Kalceni base, I want you to plot a course."

"Affirmative," came the reply.

The image returned to the star chart, and Onlor gazed directly at the core worlds the Kalceni once called home. He could only hope whatever they found was more intact than what they found at the base.

FIFTEEN

Chancellor's Estate - Morballo Prime

Chancellor Hathdal sat behind his desk, transfixed on the holographic image before him. The map representing the space between the Trevien and Quaron star systems was nothing unusual, but it was the several tinier blips facing off against each another between the two regions which held his attention.

"This is an up-to-date look at the Trevien and Quaron fleet movements that came through to headquarters this morning," Supreme Commander Bostax said, standing next to the hologram in front of the desk. "It would appear both powers have gathered their forces on what would once have been considered their border."

Hathdal shook his head. "How did this happen?"

His main political advisor, Tiron, remained in his seat in the darkest corner of the room. "Intelligence reports that both sides have grievances with one another. The Treviens claim the Quarons destroyed one of their freighters, while the Quarons maintain the Treviens attacked one of their warships."

"Have any of these claims been substantiated?"

"A nearby Alliance patrol attempted to investigate the situation," Bostax said, "but while they were helping the disabled Quaron vessel, word filtered through from their governments that our ships were to leave the area immediately."

Hathdal stood and walked around his desk, looking closely at the holographic scans. "On what grounds?"

"They cited the Alliance Independence Act," Tiron interjected. "It allows local governments to suspend all external traffic through their star systems for a limited period."

"I know what the Independence Act is," Hathdal grumbled. "What I want to know is how this could have happened."

"I can't answer that, but there's little doubt they want to fight it out." Bostax altered the image, bringing up closer scans of the ships on either side of the brewing conflict. "Each fleet wields significant arsenals."

"Legally, how long until we can send an Alliance taskforce in?"

Tiron got out of his seat to join the others around the desk. "They have a week."

"And there's no loophole around that?"

"Not unless you want to break Alliance law."

"In a week there might be nothing left of the Treviens or Quarons." Hathdal frowned and returned to his chair. "Centuries ago, before they became members of the Alliance, they'd been at war with each other for decades. Generations on both sides went to battle. Most never returned. Those that did come home, came back with stories of how barbaric the other side was. Even hundreds of years of peace under the banner of the Alliance can't alter the trials of those days."

Tiron moved to the left-hand side of his desk and leaned on the old wooden slab transported from Hathdal's planet the day he'd been made chancellor. "As heartless as it sounds, unfortunately the Treviens and the Quarons are the least of our worries. I've been receiving reports throughout the Alliance of issues arising due to food shortages, supply chain shutdowns, medical supply theft, and worker strikes."

"And let me guess." Hathdal turned to his Supreme Commander. "With your fleet still rebuilding from the Kalceni attack, your forces have been stretched too thin to take care of it?"

Bostax nodded.

"Things are unravelling quicker than we can handle," Tiron continued.

Hathdal glanced out the window behind him at the place he'd called home. Morballo Prime was a long way from the planet where he was born, but going there was a necessity if anyone ever wanted to enter public office and serve the greater good. After so many decades of plying his trade in the enormous hall that was the home of the Alliance Council across the river, he couldn't have foreseen such a crisis unfolding. The Alliance was founded as a beacon of hope for the entire galaxy, but since the Kalceni attack, it was as if something had pulled at the fabric of all the good it had achieved.

He steepled his fingers on his desk. "Then it looks like we've got a lot of work to do. I want a meeting with every ambassador, starting tomorrow morning. I don't care how long it takes. We'll start with those with the highest amount of grievances. Supreme Commander, I'd like you to send a liaison from headquarters to this office every two hours, updating me on everything you have. Let's put a stop to this before it gets out of hand."

Bostax switched off the hologram. "As you wish, Chancellor."

Hathdal turned to Tiron, but before he could give him any instructions, the door to office opened and his assistant appeared. "I'm sorry to disturb you, Chancellor, but Ambassador Inzarto's here to see you."

Hathdal shared an uneasy glance with his advisor. "That will be all, Supreme Commander."

His highest military officer bowed and exited the office, passing by his assistant on the way out.

"Okay, send her in," Hathdal instructed her.

His assistant stepped aside, and the tall lithe figure from the planet Cuneris entered, walking by Tiron and taking up a position in front of the desk. Hathdal nodded at his assistant, and she closed the door behind her.

"Ambassador Inzarto, it's good to see you. I was just discussing, with my advisor here, that it was beyond time I sat down with all the representatives of the Alliance to discuss current events."

"I'm here to deliver a message," she said bluntly.

Hathdal narrowed his eyes at her abruptness. While he didn't mind testy conversations with those beneath him, usually his office garnered a little more respect before things got heated. "What can I do for you, Ambassador?"

"I come to you as a courtesy before the Alliance Council meeting tomorrow afternoon." She pulled out an old paper scroll.

Hathdal almost chuckled, forgetting the last time he'd seen something of such antiquity.

"When the Alliance was founded, my world, yours, and the one we currently stand on, all agreed to unite and forge a great relationship for the betterment of our races. That association blossomed in the decades and centuries to come to form the Alliance we know today. This parchment was signed to signify our worlds' entry and has been displayed in our finest museum ever since." She placed the scroll on his desk. "You're obviously aware of the referendum that has gone before the people of Cuneris. They had two options. To remain in the Alliance, or secede and become whole again as an independent world."

Hathdal's legs quivered. He pushed himself farther under the desk to ensure she couldn't see his weakness. "Ambassador, I—"

"Chancellor," Inzarto interrupted. "The votes have been cast, and the decision made. The delegates of my world have sent me here to inform you that as of tomorrow afternoon at the Alliance Council chambers, Cuneris will announce its secession from the Alliance."

Hathdal didn't know what to say. He'd made a career of being able to fill a hole in a conversation as the skilled politician he was born to be. Ambassador Inzarto didn't give him a chance to blurt something out, instead bowing and leaving his office.

Tiron moved in front of his desk, and his long shadow appeared over Hathdal and the parchment between them. "No world in all the centuries of the Alliance has ever seceded." There was panic in the man's voice, something Hathdal had never heard before.

"Don't you think I know that." He allowed his calm exterior to crack for a moment and slammed his fist on his desk.

"With Cuneris seceding, it may open the floodgates for more planets to look inward," Tiron continued. "If the Alliance splinters, there's no telling what it could do. War on hundreds of fronts isn't out of the question."

Hathdal unclenched his fist as marks appeared on his hand. "Ironic, isn't it?"

Tiron furrowed his brow. "Chancellor?"

"Even the Kalceni could not have foreseen the destruction we can inflict on each other. Perhaps they didn't need their weapon ship after all." Hathdal stared at the parchment, noting how fragile it was and how easily it could crumble.

Just like the Alliance...

SIXTEEN

Gunos

Susan Tai directed her mobility chair down the ramp of the transport vessel and stopped at the bottom, letting the cool breeze flutter her hair. She put her hand above her eyes to shield the glare from the setting binary suns, and through it, spotted the entrance to the Gunosien Capital Hospital. It was one of the most beautiful structures she'd ever seen. Painted in white, it was more akin to the stylish opera houses she'd occasionally frequented back on Earth.

Behind her, the ramp retracted, and the transport ship rose into the air. It created an even stronger breeze, forcing Susan to move toward the hospital. Just as she was about to make her way through the entrance, three figures emerged. All smiled warmly at her, but it was the one at the center who she noticed more than the others. His expression was so infectious that she couldn't help but smile back.

"Hello, Doctor Tai. Welcome to my home." He put his hands in the air. "We're glad you finally made it."

"It's good to see you, Doctor Iarinos," she said. "It feels like an eternity since our last meeting."

He gestured to the pair beside him. "This is Doctor Teklar and Doctor Majooh. They'll be assisting me in your surgery."

Susan nodded at the two women, representing a species she'd been yet to meet. Both had pale white skin and eyes as blue as the Gunosien sky. Their hair was thickly braided, and so blonde, it was almost yellow.

"Well," Iarinos continued, "would you like to see the hospital?"

The group set off and entered the building into the bustling hive of activity one would expect with any kind of major medical facility. The ceiling was so high it seemed to disappear into the sun gleaming through the numerous glass windows, while all the different levels were connected by gorgeous spiral staircases and a series of elevators. It almost reminded her of the TIAS building in Tokyo but more elaborate. However, even though it was grandiose, there was a homeliness about it, which differed from similar facilities back in the commonwealth, which far too often were cold and sterile.

"I've never seen anything like this," she said to the first face she remembered seeing after the destruction of the Kalceni weapon ship.

"This is the main hospital on my world," Iarinos informed her. "Nothing comes close in terms of size and scope. There are smaller clinics scattered throughout

Gunos, but this is where all the major surgeries take place. We find the calming environment here helps the healing process of those that enter our doors."

Susan stopped at the bottom of the enormous winding staircases, linking at least a dozen stories above the ground level. She couldn't help but be in awe at the breathtaking architecture. "I bet there's a nice view from up there."

She'd gotten a glimpse of the capital city on the journey down from orbit, just before touching down on the hospital's landing deck. It was beauty on a scale she'd seen only very few times before.

"You'll get to see it when you're out of surgery, and might even get to walk those stairs yourself if you're feeling up to it." Iarinos motioned toward the elevator, and the party of four entered.

The elevator carriage came to a halt at their destination, and the doors opened. Doctors and nurses hurried about in surgical gowns before them, portraying a much more businesslike setting. The circular space was still inviting, but there was a professionalism and a reinforcement that Susan was truly where she needed to be.

Doctor Iarinos led her to the heart of the facility, where a massive bank of computers displayed medical readings from the thousands of patients in the hospital's care. Susan would have once wanted to ask many questions. The scientist in her was never satisfied, but for the first time in so very long she was content to take in her surroundings in fascination. She wasn't sure whether it was the fatigue of her trip or the fact she knew she was so close to a life-changing surgery.

The image of Nicolas back on the *Argo* after rescuing him from Rixiia entered her mind. The frail body taken by Jung's Disease was hard to forget, along with the last moments she'd got to share with him. A guilt festered inside her at the thought of being finally healed, while the man she'd called the love of her life was long dead.

"Doctor Tai?"

She turned to her friend and attempted to blink away the tears swelling up in the corner of her eyes. "I'm sorry. I was just..."

Iarinos walked toward her. "Are you okay?"

Another memory flashed by of her wedding day, and the enormous smile on Nicolas's face when he'd uttered the timeless words, 'I do.'

"Yes." Susan smiled, but she wasn't able to stop a tear from dropping down her cheek.

Iarinos looked at her with a crooked brow. "Are you sure?"

She nodded, and the doctor led her to a room branching off from the huge center. The confines were tiny compared to anywhere else she'd seen on her visit. Apart from a peculiar bed in the middle of it, the room was basically empty.

"This is a medical tube." Iarinos waved at the bed, which seemed similar to a stasis chamber. "This is where the magic will happen. Due to the complexity of this surgery, we won't be cutting into your skin in the traditional sense, rather we'll use an electromagnetic system to pinpoint coordinates inside your body to alter remotely."

Susan had already been briefed on everything her friend had told her but appreciated the courtesy of him repeating it. She was impressed with the concept of the surgery and hoped once she was back on her feet again she'd get to pick Iarinos's brain to gain more knowledge about the advanced type of procedure.

He moved toward the tube, which to the naked eye appeared little more than a hollow shell of nothingness. There wasn't so much as a panel or circuitry of any kind within it. "Now, I must warn you, it won't be as simple as going in and out of the tube to be able to walk again. When you emerge, you'll almost certainly have feeling back in your legs, but the link between your top and lower half won't be completely reconnected. You'll want to take your first steps, but it'll take time. Patience will be a virtue."

Susan wiped her eyes and rid herself of any lingering tears.

"Are you ready?" the doctor asked her.

SEVENTEEN

Vantar

"Would you check this out?"

As Jason walked down the rear entry ramp of the *Argo*, the scale and immensity of the splendid vista revealed itself. On one side of the vast landing pad was a beach looking out onto a purple ocean which sprawled all the way to the horizon. On the other side were the tallest and greenest trees he'd ever seen in his life. Just when he thought he'd seen all the beauty in the universe, the galactic gods continued to provide.

Everyone aboard the *Argo* was desperate for a layover. Their experience with the Trevien freighter and the Quarons had put a real downer on their time working in the Alliance. Being able to bask in the planet's magnificence would hopefully allow them to leave the incident well behind them.

Mirin prepared the cargo for unloading, while Aly and Kevin helped get the hover lifters out of storage. Althaus, too, unable to stop himself, stumbled around on his crutches, double-checking the inventory. Jason gave his crewmates a helping hand and grabbed a hover lifter of his own, pulling the first container from the ship and placing it on the landing pad, ready for their buyer to come and collect.

It didn't take them long to empty the shipment, which was impressive considering how full their hold was. But he, like everyone else, no doubt wanted to get the job done so they could enjoy some much-needed rest. They locked the *Argo* down, then went and found the nearest local establishment, which conveniently was right on the beach, resembling something akin to a tiki bar. All that was missing were the hula girls.

Jason led them to a table so close to the water that he worried when the tide came in, they'd be washed away. The locals simply laughed, informing him the water was always calm on their world. Trusting the native Vantarian knowledge, he took Kevin with him to the bar to collect some drinks. While they waited, the *Argo's* helmsman examined Jason as if he were a patient in his infirmary.

"You've been quiet lately," he noticed.

"Have I?" Jason played with a swizzle stick someone had left on the bar. "I wasn't aware."

"You're still thinking about what happened to the Treviens, aren't you?"

"It's hard to forget what we saw."

"True. But we've seen a lot, especially in the last few years." Kevin put his hand in a bowl of a Vantarian snack which looked like miniature peanuts. He threw a few in his mouth. "What made this so different?"

Jason snapped the swizzle stick in half. "I don't know exactly. I suppose I've been thinking about what that cleric said on Mascoros Prime."

"The Firstborn?"

Jason nodded.

Kevin grabbed a napkin and spat out the peanuts, screwing up his face. "That cleric sounded like a bit of a kook to me."

"So did the one on Tadrosia. You remember him, right?"

The older man chuckled. "I remember."

"The prophecy he told of the Guardian coming to save them, was in fact Kione destroying the weapon ship."

"Prophecies can be twisted to mean anything when you break them down."

"True, but think about who the Retebu are. Or who they were. The sphere was effectively a time capsule for their species, and Kione, a being who has evolved to the point that his form is completely different to our own. Perhaps those prophecies are in fact what's actually coming, because the people who wrote them have already witnessed the events."

Kevin stared blankly at him. "You're thinking too much."

"No one has ever accused me of that before."

The Vantarian behind the bar handed them two

trays of drinks. Jason gathered one and set off to the table to the others, while Kevin followed.

"What's all this?" Aly's eyes widened as large as dinner plates at the shot glasses on Jason's tray.

He plonked it down on the center of the table and handed one of the neon-red drinks to everyone. "The barman called this—"

"Fireburn." Mirin took her glass and held it up. It was almost luminescent in the establishment's light. "This is the most potent alcoholic beverage in the Alliance."

"What are you trying to do?" Aly said. "Kill us?"

Jason grabbed the glass of water from Kevin's tray and placed it in front of her. "Your chaser."

She rolled her eyes.

"I thought we all needed to let our hair down." He put his hand up to stop Aly before she could rebut him. "Special occasions."

"And what special occasion is this?" Althaus asked.

"Still being alive." Jason stared around the table at his crewmates. No one complained. Not even Aly, who placed the fireburn in her hand. He took a seat, joining the others, and raised his shot glass in the air. "To the best crew any cargo captain could ever ask for."

Everyone smiled. Even Althaus, who seemed to do everything in his power to stop himself. They all drew back their glasses and swallowed the red liquid.

The next thing Jason remembered was flinging the glass onto the tray and howling like a werewolf. Althaus slammed his fist against the table, while Aly glugged down her water and Kevin gasped for some air beside her. Mirin was the only one who seemed to take the throat-burning alcohol without it nearly making her sick. Jason turned to her, allowing the end of his tongue to stop tingling.

"I'm guessing that wasn't your first glass of fire-burn?" he said.

A smirk appeared, and Mirin shrugged as everyone recovered, taking their requested drinks from the other tray and chugging them down. Jason wanted to apologize to them, but before he could utter a word from his dry mouth, a voice rang out over the establishment's speakers.

"This is an emergency announcement."

Everyone stopped, and a holographic Vantarian appeared before the bar, dressed in a nice suit.

"Who's that?" Jason asked.

"That's Vantar's Premier Official," Mirin said.

"So, like their president?"

"Effectively. She's voted in by the Vantarian people and elects an ambassador to speak for her before the Alliance Council."

"I come to you today with news from Morballo Prime," the Premier Official began. *"This afternoon, Cuneris, a founding member of the Alliance, have announced they are seceding from our sprawling coalition of planets."*

Audible gasps went up around the bar, as many of the different crews of cargo jockeys looked at each other in shock.

"Other worlds of the Alliance are beginning consultation with their own citizens. On Vantar, it would be irresponsible to not go through a similar process. I implore you to all remain calm in the following days and weeks. Your government officials will inform you of any new developments."

The hologram faded, and those in the bar remained silent. A few seconds later, a massive wave of noise went up as conversations started breaking out.

Jason glanced at Kevin, and their wary eyes met. "Maybe those clerics were onto something after all."

EIGHTEEN

Cargo Ship Argo

Aly stopped on the bridge and plonked her tool kit on the captain's chair. She gazed out at Vantar's beauty beyond the landing pad, a place she was happy to call home, for at least a little while until they blasted back out into space for their next job.

Normally after a job well done, she was in the most upbeat of moods. Everyone was. Even Althaus. Kind of. But since their run-in with the Quarons and the news of a major Alliance member seceding, there was only gloom. The whole crew sensed it. Especially Jason, who remained quite guarded.

Aly opened her tool kit and rifled through it to find her handheld scanner to begin much-needed maintenance of the bridge consoles. While her father had done a reasonable job putting them back together after the incident with the Quarons, a lighter touch was required to keep them operating at peak efficiency. She went to the helm first and lifted the external casing, revealing the inner components. Some were burned out, while others were only running due to the auxiliary circuits taking over.

She sat and let out a loud sigh. Embarrassed, she looked around to make sure the bridge was still empty. As she was about to install the first component, the operations station bleeped from the starboard side of the bridge. Aly trudged over to the station to check out the incoming commlink to find a communiqué in the form of a text message had been sent through to them.

"Uh-oh."

"Jason?"

Aly walked to the door to her quarters and pushed it open, but when she entered, all she found was an empty chair behind Jason's shabby desk. She went back out into the B Deck corridor, wondering if he was down in the cargo bay. She made her way to the elevator but stopped at the soft sound of water pitter-pattering.

She spun around and went inside the *Argo's* bathroom facilities. "Jason, is that you in there?" Aly asked outside the running shower cubicle.

A head bobbed up from over the screen, but only enough for her to see the tops of his eyes. "I'm here," he said. "What's up?"

Jason opened the screen ever so slightly, trickling some water onto her boots.

"Don't you dare!" she quipped, slamming it shut.

Jason chuckled.

"I don't want to dampen the mood, but a message just came through from the Commonwealth Shipping Network," she informed him.

The tap squeaked, and the water stopped flowing from the showerhead. He opened the screen and stepped out, completely naked. Aly threw him a towel to cover up his modesty and handed him her data tablet. She tried to read all the expressions on his face as he read the message. Strangely, he was quite calm.

"I assume you've got everyone gathered together?" he asked.

"They'll be up in the galley in five minutes."

Jason got dressed, and the pair rode the elevator to A Deck, where the rest of the crew were waiting. Mirin and Althaus were sitting next to each other at table, while Aly's dad fixed himself a coffee at the counter.

"What is it?" her father asked almost immediately, no doubt sensing something was up.

Jason tossed the data tablet on the table. "We've been ordered home."

Althaus grabbed it and scanned over the message.

"Essentially, as far as the Commonwealth Shipping Network are concerned, the Alliance is no longer safe for trading operations," Jason continued. "They won't insure us and are directing all cargo ships back to commonwealth territory."

"This is an advisory notice." Althaus held the tablet aloft and passed it to Aly's dad.

"We've all seen firsthand what's happening out here. The Alliance is crumbing. From everything we're hearing, more worlds are looking to secede, which means trade is going to become much more difficult. And more dangerous."

"Jason's right."

They all turned to the one person who was yet to say anything. And it was the one person who was most qualified to speak. "In all my life I never thought I'd witness something like this," Mirin said. "I fear the Alliance might be at a point where there will be no way back."

"I suppose I should play devil's advocate here," Aly interjected. "Mirin, what would happen if we were to go against the CSN's advice and remain out here?"

"I can't say for certain, but the clouds of war are gathering across many fronts. You could well find yourself between several battlefronts with no way of getting home." She frowned. "If the Alliance splinters and worlds form smaller alliances amongst themselves, there's no knowing what could happen. And then there's the gateway network. It'll go from being centrally controlled, to being at the mercy of the local authorities who no longer call themselves Alliance citizens. You could face roadblocks wherever you go."

"I don't particularly like the idea of paying tolls or pledging fealty just to transit the trans-space corridors." Jason leaned on the back of a spare chair. "And it's not like we have our own trans-space engine. Even if we did, we'd only need to find ourselves in the wrong place at the wrong time and..."

He drifted off, and Aly walked up beside him, putting her hand on his arm. "We've been in tough spots before."

"We have, but sometimes we have to know our limitations." He peered deep into her eyes. "We have to go home while we can. If we lose access to the gateway network, we may never get back."

"Shouldn't we at least discuss this more? We could—"

"The kid's right," Althaus interrupted her. "I mean, Jason's right. The *Argo* might have some shields now, but we'll still be way over our heads out here if we come across someone like the Quarons again."

Aly wanted to keep pushing, but she caught a glimpse of her father as he placed his mug on the table.

"I'm afraid I have to agree," the sage old Rycroft said. "There's no harm in returning to the commonwealth. The current climate in the Alliance might blow over. There's nothing stopping us from coming back when it has."

"Well, what about Mirin?" Aly asked.

"You can drop me off somewhere on your journey back through the gateway network," their alien crew member told her. "From there I can get transport to where I need to go."

Jason put his hands on his hips. "Thanks, everyone. Kevin, once we're ready, take us into orbit and set course for Vantar's gateway."

Aly's father nodded, and Jason walked out of the

galley. Aly rushed after him and grabbed him by the arm, stopping him in his tracks.

"What was all that about?" she asked.

Jason furrowed his brow. "What do you mean?"

"You love it out here. Surely you don't want to go back to the commonwealth?"

"Not really, but I don't particularly like the idea of dodging potshots out here, while the galaxy goes to hell in a handbasket either."

"So, you're giving up?"

"What would you have me do? I've got a crew to protect." He peeled her arms from him and took her by the hand. "I've got you to protect."

She froze. "This is about me?"

His cheeks reddened. "This is about everyone. We're not invincible. Sometimes, we just have to know when to sit on the sidelines."

And with that, he continued back off down the corridor and disappeared onto the bridge.

NINETEEN

Swirls of light and dark surrounded Susan, and her head spun with the rhythmic movements of the weird colors finally taking shape ahead of her.

The Vanguard?

The corridors of the ship she'd once served aboard were eerily quiet. With the night turning into morning, everyone was either getting some shuteye or playing a game of cards and a having a sneaky drink at the end of their watches.

Susan trudged on, remembering the day as if it were yesterday and reliving the horrors she'd witnessed. Just that afternoon the *Vanguard* and its battle group were taken by surprise and ambushed by Centauri forces. They managed to repel the enemy, but one CDF vessel was lost and another severely damaged. Once the skirmish ended, Susan and her medical team went over to the ship to aid them in their efforts. Many had already died, and several were badly wounded.

She stopped at the corner of the corridor and froze, trying to push the images in her mind aside. Her hands shook, and she placed them in her pocket. It did little to calm her nerves. She almost felt like a first-year medical student again.

This damn war...

Susan carried on to the ship's sickbay and put on the demeanor required of her as she entered. The beds were full of wounded from the *Vanguard*, along with a few more from the other ships in the battle group. Her staff appeared just as weary as her but continued their work without complaint. She nodded at the few who looked her way and pressed on to her office.

Stacks of paperwork in the form of data tablets awaited her. She plopped herself down behind her desk and fell into the back of her chair, closing her eyes, trying to forget about everything, even if just for a few seconds.

"Hello, Susan."

She allowed her eyelids to slowly open to find Nicolas's familiar figure standing at the door in his disheveled uniform.

The man known as Captain Marquez to the rest of the crew walked over the threshold and stopped in front of her desk. "I'm sorry. I know I probably shouldn't have come. But when I heard you'd got back from the *Sherman*, I..."

Susan smiled. It didn't last long, but she appreciated the happiness it bought her, nonetheless. "Don't be silly."

He took a seat on the edge of the desk and rubbed his temples.

"Are we in the clear?" she asked him.

"There's been no more enemy contacts on the scanners." He stared through the transparent screen, out at the wounded in her sickbay. "In open space, I don't expect we'll find ourselves foul of a Centauri surprise attack again."

"There's no way you could have known. We needed to pass by that star system. It was just bad luck that we stumbled upon a hive of the Centauri hiding inside it."

"Yeah." His eyes didn't waver from the injured crew members. "It doesn't make what happened any easier. We lost a lot of good people today."

She reached for his hand, and they both held on to each other tight.

"I love you, Susan," he said, turning to her.

"Words I could never get sick of."

"That's a relief, because..." Nicolas reached his other hand into his pocket. "I had planned to do this somewhere else. Somewhere away from all of this. But I can't wait any longer. Not after what happened today." He hopped off the desk and got down on one knee, revealing a stunning gold ring. "This was my great-great grandmother's."

She gazed at the light twinkling in the beautiful diamond on top of the ring, and her hands once again quaked.

"Susan Tai, will you marry me?" Nicolas asked.

Before she could answer, the *Vanguard's* sickbay

disappeared, and she found herself back on Earth. More precisely, her husband's memorial in Miami. Years had flashed by, and before her, men in CDF uniforms fired off a twenty-one gun salute.

Others gathered around, civilians and defense force personnel alike. And before them lay the casket, representing Nicolas, with the flag of the United Earth Commonwealth draped over it. As was tradition, a pair of young officers folded it and handed it to Susan while she sat taking in the service from her mobility chair. They saluted, and a CDF transport pod flew overhead. The noise jangled her bones. At least those she could still feel.

Then her eyes burst open.

She wasn't on the *Vanguard*. Or on Earth.

Darkness surrounded her.

Where am I?

Susan put her hands out, and they stopped only centimeters from her face. And that's when it hit her.

Gunos?

She brushed the inside of the medical tube with her hand and tried to push it ajar. But it wouldn't budge.

"Doctor Iarinos?" she called out.

He didn't reply.

Susan rolled on her shoulder to one side, and then the other, to find an escape. Near her waist, she found a latch. She yanked at it, and a gentle hiss of air whistled around her. The tube slowly opened, revealing the interior of the surgical bay in the Gunosien Capital Hospital.

"Doctor Iarinos, are you there?" she shouted again. "Can anyone hear me?"

With no reply, she drove her hands into the bed and heaved herself into an upright position, finding the surgical bay completely empty. The lighting was darker than before, too. Susan peered at the floor, which seemed so far down. But then her instincts kicked in and she shifted toward the edge of the tube, but not with the muscles in the top of her body, rather the ones beneath her waist.

"Oh my god," she uttered as her thighs moved to the side. It wasn't just the slight movement that caught her off guard, but the feeling. It might have been dulled, but there was definitely a sensation in the bottom half. She peered at her naked toes and concentrated. Then one by one, every one of them on her left foot wiggled.

A smile curled at the edge of her mouth, and a surge of adrenaline pulsated through her. "Doctor Iarinos. I'm ready to come out now."

But her friend didn't answer again. Neither did any of his staff. Susan looked back down at her legs. She remembered Iarinos telling her she wouldn't be able to walk right away, and that it would take time to get used to the process. Being a doctor herself, she obviously understood the muscle loss that came with being hit with the Kalceni energy weapon. But after the initial movements she'd experienced, she wondered if she might be more advanced than once thought. There was only one way to find out.

Susan dangled her legs over the edge of the medical

tube and took a deep breath. She threw herself from the bed and landed with her feet first. Neither of them stuck, however, and she tumbled to the floor. Every part of her body ached, including the lower half. The adrenaline in her system helped her onward, however, and she crawled across the carpet, using the strength in her upper body.

She dragged herself to the door, and it opened into the main center she'd visited before being taken into surgery. The vast banks of computers at the heart of the room were still operating. But, like the surgical bay, there wasn't a soul in sight.

"Hello!"

This time her echo bounced off the walls, so she plowed on. Tingles permeated in and around her shoulders, and she struggled under the strain. Luckily, her upper body was much stronger than it ever had been, and she could continue taking a pounding, regardless.

Through the opening, she went to find a railing at the edge. She stopped at the bottom and pulled herself up, one rung at a time, until she was standing on her own two feet again. It was a completely different perspective. One she hadn't seen for so very long. But before she could congratulate herself, she gazed out through giant windows at the view of the city beyond, which she'd so wanted to see when she'd first arrived at the hospital.

But where she expected to find a sprawling metropolis standing, it was instead engulfed in flames.

Fighter crafts flew over it, discharging energy weapons on the populace below. Suddenly, her feet gave way, and she fell to the floor again with a thud.

What the hell's going on here?

TWENTY

Brielaro

Javier walked into his own personal confines aboard the Company vessel and breathed a sigh of relief at the bed in the far corner of his quarters. It wasn't in the state he would have liked, neglecting to tidy up that morning, but due to the sheer size of the room, it didn't matter if he had to step over a few things.

The door closed behind him, and he sat at the desk in front of his holographic computer. While he conducted most of his studies in the lab, five decks down, from time to time he longed for the solitude of working alone. But now wasn't the moment. He peered through the viewport at the trans-space corridor as the *Brielaro* charged to the Kalceni home world. Or at least what he assumed was once its location. The spinning colors of the Iota particles creating the intergalactic tunnel made him yearn that much more for slumber.

He checked the chronometer above the bed and

raised his eyebrows, remembering something he should have done much earlier. He swiveled in his chair and activated the holographic controls. They came to life full of color, and he prepared to open a commlink.

"Attempting communiqué with Gunos," the computer informed him.

A circular holographic symbol spun around for what seemed like an eternity. It then stopped and flashed red.

"Unable to complete task. All communications in and out of the Gunos system have been suspended."

"Explain," Javier demanded.

"Explanation unknown."

The computer closed down, and Javier scratched his chin. In no mood for mysteries, he got out of his chair and left the quarters, making his way to the *Brielaro's* bridge. As it was evening, the ship's command center was relatively quiet, but luckily for him, a familiar face was still on duty at the communications station.

"Kranlar." He stopped by the younger man, who was the same species as Onlor.

"Good evening, Professor. What can I do for you?" the Ulvekan asked.

"I need a favor."

"Don't you always?"

Javier grinned. "I just tried to send a communiqué to the Gunos. I have a friend who was having surgery at their main hospital, and I wanted to see how she was recovering. For some reason, I couldn't contact her."

Kranlar looked sideways for a moment. "I have a feeling I know why that is."

"Oh?"

"Last information I saw on that region of space reported a joint Xanian and Olopan fleet heading toward the Gunos star system."

"Are they members of the Alliance?"

"Yes. Well, actually no. They were until their planets seceded."

"Seceded?" Javier sat on the console next to him and furrowed his brow.

"Have you not been keeping up to date, Professor?"

"Apparently not. What's been happening?"

"A few days ago, Cuneris announced its secession, and it's since caused other worlds to join them in abandoning the Alliance." Kranlar frowned. "Some are going it alone, while others are creating smaller coalitions based on old rivalries that were in effect before the founding of the current organization we know today."

Javier wasn't quite sure what to say. "I guess I've had my head in my work so much, I haven't stopped long enough to see what else had been going on."

"I've been thinking about my world constantly. It's far away from where most of the problems are arising, but who knows what will happen in the future."

"You've got a wife and child back home, haven't you?" Javier said, remembering previous conversations they'd had during their voyage.

Kranlar nodded. "They have a safe place to go if it comes to it."

Javier grasped his shoulder, thinking of the poor man and his family. "I don't wish to sound heartless, Kranlar, but I need to know more about Gunos."

"There's not much to tell you, Professor. I'm not aware of the finer details, but for many years the Xanians and Olopans have been disputing mining contracts near their systems which have traditionally been under the control of the Gunosiens. Usually, the arguments have been mediated by the Alliance Council and compromises found. But lately, there's a perception the Alliance is weak."

"Is that why all these planets are seceding?"

"Perhaps." Kranlar turned in his chair and placed one leg over the other to get more comfortable. "The Xanians and the Olopans are obviously fed up with how everything's been handled and are looking to take matters into their own hands."

"So, they've aligned against the Gunosiens?"

The Company officer nodded. "With the Alliance military in such a state of disrepair after the Kalceni attack, it'll be difficult to stop these spot fires. Similar stories like this one are popping up all over the Alliance."

While Javier was horrified and intrigued by the situation, he felt guilty he had only one person on his mind. "What do you think might happen to my friend?"

"I wish I could say." Kranlar leaned closer to him, keeping his voice down. "If the Xanians and Olopans intend to invade Gunos, let's just say I wouldn't want to be in her shoes right now. Neither is a race to get on the wrong side of. And with the shackles off..."

The Company officer drifted off, and Javier stared back out at the trans-space corridor, just as fixated on the magnificent mixture of colors as he had been earlier. His fatigue gave way to the memories he'd shared with Susan Tai from the moment he'd met her at the Tokyo Advanced Institute of Sciences, to the time they were thrown across the galaxy together on a quaint old cargo ship.

"I need your assistance with something, Kranlar, if you're able?" Javier asked.

"I'll do anything I can to help," he assured him.

"Good. I want you to send a message for me."

"Of course. Who do you want it sent to?"

"Well, I can tell you who to send it to, but we'll have to track them down first."

"Don't worry, that's where I excel." Kranlar put his hands on his console. "Take a seat, Professor."

TWENTY-ONE

Cargo Ship Argo

Jason stumbled onto the bridge and staggered toward the helm, falling into the seat. With his weary eyes he gazed at the trans-space corridor surrounding the *Argo* as it swirled around him.

Not wanting to vomit, he rested his head against the controls, being careful not to touch anything that might send the ship off course. Before he could close his eyelids, a strange noise filtered through the hatchway. He pulled himself up and stood, making his way out into the A Deck corridor, and stopping by the door to the rec room.

The sofa in the corner was occupied with Althaus's sturdy frame stretched out over it. Over the speakers, a style of music, at least thirty years before Jason's time, played out. He wanted to ask him what it was but didn't wish to disturb him. It wasn't often he found Althaus by himself in the rec room, and even rarer to see him listening to music. Jason wondered if recent events had affected his uncle as much as him.

He moved on and stopped again as another figure emerged from the galley on the other side of the corridor. The man sipped his coffee and looked at Jason with a crooked gaze.

"You've been drinking," Kevin noticed.

Jason leaned against the bulkhead, doing everything in his power to not fall over. "Well, that bottle I brought back from Vantar was just asking to be drunk."

"Where is it?"

Jason blushed. "Uh, I'm pretty sure I finished it."

Kevin frowned, doing what he usually did, trying not to show his dissatisfaction. "Where's Alyssa?"

"She went to bed. I think she was a little pissed at me."

"I don't doubt it."

"I should probably go to bed, too. Maybe if I apologize now, she won't be so pissed with me tomorrow."

A small grin appeared on Kevin's face. "Anything's possible."

Jason grasped the man's shoulder, thanking him for forgoing any lectures, and set off down the elevator to B Deck. Rather than stopping at his destination, the car continued to C Deck. He checked the controls and discovered he'd accidentally set it to the lowest level of the *Argo*. When he reached the bottom, instead of returning up the shaft, he walked out into the cargo bay and stood in the center of the ship's empty hold.

Every step he took echoed against the bulkheads,

creating a distinct sensation of loneliness. He couldn't remember the last time the cargo bay was so bare. Jason thought about everything that had happened and wondered what waited for them on their return to Earth. It would probably be just like before, when humanity was shut off from the rest of the galaxy. He didn't want to be that teenager he once was, so desperately wanting to leave the *Argo*.

But then again, things are different this time, aren't they?

A clang sounded from behind, and he spun around to the *Julieanne's* airlock. He craned his neck at the entrance into the *Argo's* transport pod and traipsed over to it with his wobbly legs.

"Hello?" he called out.

No one answered.

"Is anyone in here?" he asked again.

Something else clattered inside, and a shadow moved in front of him against the inner bulkhead of the craft. He entered, and someone appeared from the darkness.

"Jason!"

Mirin stepped into the light emanating from the cargo bay through the airlock.

"Mirin?" he said, a little shocked. "What are you doing in here?"

"Uh..." She glanced behind her and sighed. "Come in, I'll show you."

He followed her through into the rear compartment

of the *Julieanne* to find a small mat, sitting in the middle of the deck. "What's this?"

"It's a rokei." Mirin pointed at the fabric spread. "We use it on my world to meditate."

"You meditate?"

"My people throughout history have sought to achieve a level of awareness greater than the parts of our own physical being. Legend has it, if one were to ever attain such an awareness, we could leave our body and explore our surroundings in a way that would help us connect with the universe not possible in our corporeal flesh."

Jason blinked a few times at the explanation. "I'm sorry. I didn't understand any of that. Even if I weren't drunk, I doubt I would have either."

She chuckled. "Don't worry, it's not an easy concept to grasp, especially for off-worlders."

"Has anyone from your planet achieved this 'level of awareness?'"

"Not yet."

He placed a hand on one of the *Julieanne's* bulkheads. "I apologize, that you couldn't do your meditation in your quarters. You should have told me you weren't happy with them."

"No, it's not that at all," she assured him. "It's just..."

Jason raised his eyebrows.

"I feel horrible saying this, but I've found it difficult to concentrate in my quarters. My room's next to Althaus's, and sometimes when he's sleeping deeply—"

"You can hear his snoring?"

Her face reddened. "Please don't say anything."

"But it would be so funny."

She glared at him.

He put his hands up in surrender, doing his best to keep his snickering to a minimum. "Your secret's safe with me."

She smiled and bent down to pick up her mat.

"Don't stop on my account," he told her.

"That's okay, I was finished anyway." She folded the mat in an almost perfect square, while Jason walked to the helm and sat.

"I suppose I can't blame you coming down here, it's quite peaceful," he said. "I don't think there's anywhere else on the *Argo* where you can enjoy absolute silence. The acoustics in here are pretty good, too."

"Oh?" She pulled down one of the other seats and locked it in place. "What do you play?"

"Uh." He chuckled nervously. "Well, I don't, really. I'm still a novice. My father and brother played the guitar. It's a kind of string instrument. I, uh, yeah, I'm not very good."

"Practice makes perfect."

"So they say. In this instance I'm not sure how accurate it is."

"I'd love to hear this guitar sometime."

"I wouldn't want to do damage to your hearing before you left us." Jason's jovial mood darkened at the reminder he would soon lose his newest crew member. One he'd gotten quite used to having around. "I guess it wouldn't hurt to let you have a listen before you go."

"Bridge to Jason."

Jason froze at the sound of Aly's voice filtering through his commband. "Go ahead."

"Can you come up here?" she asked

"To the bridge? What is it?"

"There's an incoming commlink you might be interested in."

"Weren't you going to bed?"

"Can you just get up here?"

Jason, not wanting to enter into a squabble in front of Mirin, invited her to the bridge with him, and the pair stopped behind Aly at the operations station.

Aly immediately turned up her nose at him. "You smell like a brewery."

"I've been described as worse," he said. "Who's trying to contact us?"

"And old friend."

An image of Professor Javier Petit appeared on the monitor, his face stretched and warped from unknown interference.

"Alyssa? Jason?" he said across the visual commlink. *"Are you receiving me?"*

Jason nodded. "Barely, Professor. Where are you?"

"That's a long story. Suffice to say I'm not anywhere in your neighborhood. I'm using a booster on a Company ship to send this message, so I'm not sure how much time we'll have."

"What can we do for you?" Aly asked, no doubt sensing Jason wasn't in any state to coordinate the discussion.

"I need a favor." Petit's commlink became even choppier. *"It's about Doctor Tai."*

His face again disappeared, and the commlink filled with static and fuzz.

"Can you clean that up, Aly?" Jason asked her.

"No, it's all on his end," she told him. "We're lucky to be receiving a transmission at all."

"Did you get any of that?" Petit said, returning to some form of semblance.

Jason and Aly shook their heads in unison while Mirin watched on with curiosity.

"Very well, I'll explain again. At last report, Doctor Tai was on Gunos, having surgery to heal her condition. I tried to contact with her, but I wasn't able to get through to her or anyone else on the planet. Apparently the Xanians and Olopans have moved against them, sending a large fleet toward their world."

"Gunos? Xanians? Olopans?" Jason glanced at Mirin, looking for answers, as the names of the different species blended into a giant mess of words.

"I know this is asking a lot," Petit continued, *"but I have no one else to turn to."*

"You want us to see if anything's happened to her," Aly said.

"If you find yourself in too much trouble—"

"Don't worry, Professor, we'll get to her," Jason assured him.

Petit nodded. *"Thank you—"*

The professor got cut off as the commlink terminated from the distance between the two ships. It only made Jason that much more curious as to where Petit was and what he was doing on a Company ship. He pushed the questions aside and turned to Mirin again. "Where's this Gunos?"

The alien gestured to the operations station. "May I?"

Aly relinquished her chair, and Mirin sat, typing into the keypad. Watching her quick hands dance over them made Jason queasy, but he kept everything down. She brought up a star chart and pointed at the different landmarks. "When we pop out of the current corridor we're in, we'll have to transfer to another gateway and ride it all the way to Gunos."

"That detours us from your drop-off point. Do you mind coming with us, or would you like us to take you somewhere else?" Aly asked her.

"I'll help you out in any way I can," she said. "We'll deal with me later."

"All right, let's do it." Jason grabbed at his temples and headed to the hatchway. "In the meantime, I'm going to go find some detox tablets."

TWENTY-TWO

Gunos

With the help of the handrail, Susan heaved herself to her feet. While her upper body was coping with the journey she'd taken from the surgical chamber, everything below the equator felt as if someone had tenderized her with a baseball bat.

She slowly staggered to the top of the beautiful staircase, which she'd first admired when Doctor Iarinos welcomed her inside the facility's entrance. Below it, the lower levels appeared just as quiet as the surgical section. Her mind jumped from one course of action to another. If she stayed on one of the highest stories, she'd surely die when the ships attacking the capital came to the hospital to finish the job. But if she went below, she'd at least have a fighting chance of escape. Knowing she had only one course of action open to her, she grabbed the handrail of the staircase and dropped her foot onto the nearest step.

Susan did everything she could not to howl out in agony, gritting her teeth while holding in every curse word in her vocabulary. She used the pain to keep her going, almost relishing it. It meant that whatever Doctor Iarinos had done to her had worked. Now it was just a matter of surviving so she could live to speak about it.

The view of the city disappeared from the tall windows as its remains came crumbling down. She wanted to sob, but her determination wouldn't let her. After what felt like an eternity, she finally arrived at the bottom of the staircase. At the very last step, her grasp slipped from the handrail and she tumbled onto her side. With a groan, she wriggled on her back, gazing above from where she'd come from.

Only that morning it would have been an impossibility to achieve such a feat. Now, under the most trying of conditions, she'd achieved something she never thought she could again. Her mind drifted to the man who'd made it possible. She wondered what had happened to Doctor Iarinos. And everyone else.

Then the floor reverberated under her, and a nearby interior glass door shook.

Footsteps?

She sat upright and peered around the emptiness.

It won't be empty for long.

She threw herself on her front and dragged herself across the floor, eyeing a door to a nearby office. She dug her fingernails into the carpet, and the pain from the movements pulsed through her body. She wanted so much to vomit but pressed on with the shaking getting that much more intense with every passing second.

Susan stopped at the door, and beads of sweat ran down her face. Gasping for air, she placed herself under the sensor. But the door wouldn't open. With nothing to grab on but the bare wall, she put both hands onto it and hoisted herself up, one finger at a time, driving herself all the way to the manual control panel.

The interior glass door continued to quake, and then it opened.

Using all the strength left in her arms, Susan slapped the panel, and the door to her refuge slid open. She fell down and threw herself in the room, just in time to hide around the corner and catch a glimpse of the soldiers marching through the other opening.

The insectoid-like species, heavily armed, passed by her with several of the hospital staff marching before them under their watchful eye. She immediately spotted the forlorn figure of Doctor Iarinos among them.

Susan wanted to jump out and help, but her body and her mind stopped her before she could do anything so foolish. She couldn't even stand, let alone go toe to toe with an ant a foot taller than her.

The soldiers forced Iarinos and his colleagues through the exit and out onto the landing pad, where a small transport pod gently touched down in front of them.

Brielaro

Javier stood on the upper platform of the bridge, peering out through the viewport. He didn't know why, but the trans-space particles combining to make their high-velocity transit possible was strangely calming. At least it used to be, before finding out about the danger Susan was in. He did his best to hide his concern, not wanting to appear unprofessional, but even Onlor, who'd been laser-beam focused since the beginning of the expedition, would have surely sensed something.

"We're approaching the coordinates," the *Brielaro's* helmsman announced.

Onlor approached his junior officer. "Take us out of the corridor."

The reds and purples of the trans-space anomaly dispersed, and the stars emerged. The Company ship's helmsman steered the vessel slightly to port, and Planet Zero filled the forward viewport. Javier grasped hold of the handrail as they entered its orbit.

The world wasn't overly dissimilar to the one in the Kappa-Magellan system. It was just as dead, and just as treacherous, while its atmospheric conditions appeared chaotic with heavy concentrations of particulates.

"What can you see down there?" Onlor asked his officer at the scanners.

Javier unclasped himself from the handrail and walked over to the Ulvekan. They both peered over the shoulder of his officer as he brought up a series of readings and images of the surface in holographic form.

"It's an oxygen-hydrogen atmosphere," the operator said. "However, there are some regions I wouldn't advise going down to without a breathing apparatus. Gravity is within acceptable parameters, but as far as organic life goes, it's just a dead rock."

Javier studied the pictures coming in. Most of the surface of Planet Zero was rock and sand. But there was something out of place. "What's that?"

The officer focused on the image of a slightly flatter region and zoomed in on a long spike pointing out of the ground.

Onlor leaned in. "Is that—?"

"I think it is," Javier agreed.

"Ruins..." they said in unison.

TWENTY-THREE

Cargo Ship Argo

Jason tapped his fingers on the edge of the armrest, perched high in the captain's chair of the *Argo*. The effects of his excessive drinking had worn off with a quick kip and an unhealthy dose of detox tablets. Unfortunately, they didn't help with the anxiety.

All the members of his crew were hard at work around him, while Mirin remained with Aly at the operations station, answering any questions she could about the Gunosien region of space. If there was anything good that had come out of Professor's Petit's request, it was that they got to hold on to their newest recruit that little bit longer. Jason just wished it hadn't come at the expense of Susan Tai's predicament.

The doctor had been a welcome addition to the *Argo* when she'd come along to help find her husband and Tyler in their quest beyond Frontier's Reach. He'd never say a nasty word about their own resident medic,

Kevin, but having an actual doctor aboard was invaluable. From coming up with a cure to the deadly disease on the Scorpius Colony, to helping Marissa during the early stages of her pregnancy, they likely wouldn't have found the two men on Rixiia without her.

"We're approaching the gateway exit," Kevin informed him from the helm.

The trans-space corridor dispersed, and the great beyond of space appeared from the center of the vortex. Kevin let their momentum ride it out, and a planet took shape ahead of them.

"Gunos?" Jason glanced at his more knowledgeable crewmate.

Mirin nodded.

"Whoa!"

Everyone on the bridge turned to Aly, and Jason jumped from his seat, joining Mirin's side behind her.

"What is it?" he asked.

"Bogies. I'm reading at least three hundred of them." She gestured to her monitor at the smattering of dots representing the alien contacts between them and the planet. She brought up detailed scans of the ships, belonging to the two distinctly different species who had banded together against the Gunosiens. Some were gunmetal gray, with spider-like wings carrying heavy weapon platforms, while the others were sleeker, painted an almost snow white, with their weapon batteries much more discreetly hidden.

"Professor Petit wasn't wrong, was he?" Jason said. "This is a hornet's nest."

"And a few of those hornets are heading our way," she told him.

"Althaus, raise our shields."

His uncle plugged in the command, and the energy shield swiftly bathed the *Argo's* hull. Ahead, five ships made a beeline for them, all with the spider-like design.

"Xanian warships," Mirin whispered.

Jason returned to his chair as the approaching vessels maneuvered toward them and surrounded the cargo ship.

"They want to talk," Aly said.

"That's at least something." Jason breathed a sigh of relief. "Open a commlink."

An image of an insect-like being with dark-brown features and antennae revealed himself on the monitor on Jason's command station.

"I am Commander J'Lon, patrol leader of the Eighteenth Xanian Battle Squad. You have entered a highly volatile area of space. State your intentions."

"I'm Jason Cassidy of the *Cargo Ship Argo*." He sat higher, to at least attempt to evoke a position of strength. "I'm here on a job to...pick up a passenger from the Gunos."

"As you can see, that will be most difficult," the opposing commander informed him. *"Along with our Olopan allies, we're conducting military drills in this sector of space."*

Invasion more like it.

Jason wanted to verbally lash the Xanian, but he couldn't afford to antagonize his opposite number. "The last thing I want to do is interfere with your drills, but it's imperative we retrieve our passenger and take her back to Earth."

J'Lon leaned in, and his unusual set of insectoid eyes examined Jason. *"I don't think you understand the situation here. We cannot allow any foreign ships in and out of Gunosien space. I will give you one last chance to turn around and reenter the gateway. If you do not, I'll have no choice but to impound your vessel and arrest your crew for trespass."*

A sense of déjà vu came over Jason from his incident with the Quarons. "Very well, Commander, we'll return to the gateway."

Aly switched off the transmission, and Jason stood, pacing behind the helm.

"I know that look..." Kevin said.

His helmsman was an intelligent man, and just like his daughter could read him like a book.

Jason made his way over to Aly and stood behind her. "Can you bring up the makeup of the Gunos?"

She put the data on the monitor, and it appeared with all the numbers he needed. Similar to most planets of its kind, it had poles at the north and south, covered in ice, and mostly uninhabited. Neither the Xanian nor Olopans were taking much notice of the regions.

"There's a lot of interference from the orbital bombardment." Aly craned her neck up at him. "You're not thinking what I think you are, are you?"

"He is," Althaus grumbled from the systems station.

Kevin swiveled back in his chair and immediately got to work on the calculations.

"What?" Mirin said. "What are we going to do?"

"The *Argo* can reach the speed of light using a tritonium-plasma reaction," Aly informed her. "It's infinitely slower than the gateways, but before we made contact with the Alliance, it was the only way humans could roam the stars. Jason is planning to use our FTL drive to bring us out directly in the Gunos atmosphere above one of their poles. With any luck, the enemy shouldn't be able to detect us due to all the interference they've been creating."

Mirin's eyes widened. "From what I understand of your FTL system, it's extremely dangerous to operate it inside a gravitation field, is it not?"

"It is," Aly said. "Even with precise calculations, you might come out of FTL at a completely different position to where you intended."

"So, in theory, we could end up in the center of the planet?"

"It's possible."

"And that's not to mention the *Argo* herself," Althaus said from the port side of the bridge. "We try to keep atmospheric insertion to a minimum. Breaking through an atmosphere at FTL won't be easy on the ship's hull."

Jason went back to the captain's chair and sat, checking the calculations on his command station. Mirin followed and stopped next to him.

"And this is an acceptable risk to you?" she asked.

"Not exactly," he said, "but unless you have another surprise up your sleeve, we have little choice but to do things my way."

She frowned. "I wish I could say I did."

"Strap yourself in then." He put a comforting hand on her shoulder. "Kevin, how are those calculations coming?"

"We're ready to go when you are," he replied.

"We better hustle," Aly said. "The Xanians are giving us a hurry along. They want us to return to the gateway immediately."

Jason peered around the bridge, ensuring everyone was buckled in. Mirin was the last to clip herself in at one of the rear emergency seats, with a fear in her eyes Jason hadn't witnessed before. It was the first time she didn't seem to be in control. "Okay, Kevin. Hoof it!"

The *Argo* dove away from the incoming Xanian warship and engaged FTL. Space warped around them, while the stars and Gunos disappeared in a blur.

But only for a moment.

Jason didn't have a chance to enjoy the sensation of faster-than-light speed as they arrived almost instantaneously into the atmosphere of the planet. The rush of the stratosphere and the weight of the sudden gravity blasted against the hull and shook the *Argo* within an inch of its life. He could only imagine everything not bolted down in the lower decks, flying around the insides of his ship. He just hoped Kevin hadn't left his favorite coffee mug on the counter in the galley.

Below them, the ocean of Gunos appeared, and the

Argo's nose dropped and charged toward the clear blue water.

"It's time to pull up, Kevin!" Jason yelled over the din around them.

"Don't you think I know that!" His helmsman tugged at the levers and prodded at the controls.

Jason grasped the arms of his chair and braced himself.

TWENTY-FOUR

Planet Zero

The trek from the *Brielaro* to the surface of the Kalceni world drew comparisons to the first time Javier had landed on Orion V. From above, Planet Zero appeared a lot like the mining world where the Retebu sphere had been discovered. It was brown. It was rocky. And it was lifeless. At least the ride wasn't as treacherous, which was lucky because he'd just eaten lunch. When the transport pod touched down, barren plains of sand surrounded them. But there was something that broke up the very alien landscape.

Onlor pointed at the spire. "Are you coming, Professor?"

Javier broke his gaze from the viewport to find Onlor inviting him through the airlock. He followed the Ulvekan into the newly discovered environment, and its warmth immediately filled his bones. A swirling breeze rippled by and whipped up some of the sand, forcing everyone on the expedition to cover their eyes. The surface was quite soft. So soft, their boots left prints in the fine grains. But just as quickly as they were planted, the wind blew them away.

Onlor set off, leading the dozen other scientists and soldiers along with him. When they reached the alien object, Javier pulled out his handheld scanner. He almost expected it to be marble or some kind of granite, as if he were examining a lost Egyptian dig. But it was as far from the pyramids as could be possible. The long spike, at least twenty meters in length, was metallic and black.

"It's constructed of the same material found on the Kalceni base and their ships," he said.

"So, we've come to the right place." Onlor put his hands on his hips. "Widen the scope of your scanner. Let's see what else is here."

Javier did so, extending the device's range beyond a kilometer. At first all he detected were the surrounding sands, but then he calibrated it to scan the subterranean layer. "It would seem these ruins extend beneath us in every direction."

"Could we be standing on the top of what was once a Kalceni city?"

"If we are, this might have been one of the tallest buildings. Over time, what remained here was likely buried."

"The question is, is there a way in?"

Javier returned his attention to the scanner and examined the structure underneath their feet. He walked in the opposite direction and froze on a deep layer of sand. Onlor stopped behind him, and Javier pointed down. "Beneath here."

Onlor waved the rest of the expedition over to them, and shovels started appearing out of nowhere. Javier stood back while they went to work, unearthing the remains of the ancient civilization.

After what felt like hours of the Company team breaking their backs, an enormous hole was excavated before them. Below the sand, the same black smooth alloy of the spire appeared. Onlor got on his hands and knees, a little unbecoming of his position, and pushed aside the lingering grains. Javier approached as he uncovered a sealed hatch with a tiny control panel beside it.

"It doesn't look functional." He nodded to one of his nearby soldiers, and within minutes explosives were set around the antique entry.

The soldiers ushered everyone to a safe distance beyond the pit, and Onlor directed them to begin the detonation. A moment later the earsplitting explosives went off, quaking the ground beneath them. The hatch blew into the air and flew over their heads, thumping into a nearby dune.

Onlor rushed back into the pit, and Javier followed him to the hole. "Rope!"

A soldier threw a coil over the edge and held it firm with the help of one of his colleagues. Onlor grabbed hold, but in the heat of the excitement almost slipped. His right hand shook for a moment, but he quickly settled it down and dropped inside the hatchway. Javier stood in wait with the rest of the expedition while their leader's footsteps echoed inside the ruin. Javier narrowed his eyes and waved his flashlight inside, finding nothing but black.

Then from the darkness Onlor appeared, making Javier stumble backward. "Professor, get down here!"

Javier caught a glimpse of those surrounding him. Some shot him looks of scorn, others of envy. He went to the edge and clasped his hands tightly around the rope, slowly making his way down until Onlor caught him. He let go of the rope and landed on the hard floor of the Kalceni structure.

Onlor pointed his flashlight at the wall, revealing a row of Kalceni symbols. "What does it say?"

Javier aimed his flashlight at the letters. "Observation level."

"Then you were right. This must have been a building of some kind." Onlor motioned down the corridor, and they continued on. The setting was just as eerie as the Kalceni base in the Kappa-Magellan system, raising every hair on Javier's neck.

They arrived at a door and walked inside. Throughout were desks with computers on top of them, and sitting in the chairs, skeletons hunched over keypads. They had a gangly body structure and were surprisingly well-preserved.

"If these are the Kalceni, how's it possible after so many millions of years these bodies haven't decomposed?" Onlor asked.

Javier glanced at the sliver of light emanating from the exploded hatch. "We know firsthand how strong the alloy this building is constructed of. It's conceivable that whatever happened here sealed it like a tomb, limiting the amount of decay."

"And what do you surmise happened here?"

Javier reached for his scanner from his belt and pointed it at the body. "The Kalceni and the Retebu were at war—"

"Yes, but they were fighting with weapons that destroyed stars. This planet is still in one piece."

"The final conflict was waged with the power of the Retebu spheres. What we're seeing here might have been but an entrée to that conflict. An earlier war perhaps. Regardless, it's a cataclysm of planetary nature. Maybe..."

Onlor stepped closer to him. "What is it?"

Javier examined the results on his scanner. "I'm not sure yet."

"Very well." Onlor headed to the exit, but Javier lingered behind. "Let's go, Professor."

Javier took one last look at the six million year-old fossil, containing more secrets than he could know, and followed Onlor out.

TWENTY-FIVE

Gunos

Susan brushed the sweat from her forehead and stretched out her arms. While her heart rate had gone down, it hadn't stopped her from soaking her entire surgical gown with perspiration. She was lucky it wasn't as revealing as some she'd made her own patients wear back home, but it was still far from flattering and hardly appropriate for the escape she'd have to attempt.

Unfortunately, two things stood in her way. One was the aliens stalking the entrance of the facility near their transport ship on the landing pad, and the other was the increasing agony flowing through her body. Finding pain relief in a hospital wouldn't be a problem, but not when she was stuck in her small hideout.

Susan rested her head against the wall and closed her eyes, waiting for time to pass. But a muffled sound forced them open. She sat as still as she could and pressed her ear to the door.

It was a groan.

A loud one at that.

She checked the entrance of the hospital to find the alien soldiers still outside the building.

"Help me!" a distressed person called out.

Susan poked her head out as much as she dared. If she didn't know any better, she could swear the sound was coming from an alcove farther back in the lobby. She double-checked the entrance to ensure the insectoid aliens hadn't heard the cry for help. Figuring she was in the clear, she launched herself from her hiding place and dragged herself across the floor toward the suffering soul.

She pushed the glass door of the alcove ajar and hauled herself inside the small clinic. There was a solitary bed against the back wall and behind it a row of cabinets filled with drugs and medical instruments.

"Please, help!" the call howled again.

"Hello?" Susan yelled. "Are you in here?"

"I'm here!" the other person replied.

Susan followed the voice around the other side of the bed, to find a Gunosien woman sprawled face-down on the floor. She turned her head, and Susan gasped.

"Doctor Teklar!" she said to her, finding the physician in a horrible state. "What happened?"

Teklar put her hand on her side. "A Xanian got me."

"A Xanian? Those bugs?"

Teklar nodded.

Susan sat upright and shifted the doctor onto her

back, examining the bloody wound to her side. "You were struck with an energy weapon."

"Yes."

Susan placed pressure on the injury, and the memories of being hit by a similar Kalceni projectile returned to her. She glanced at the medical cabinets and latched on to the bed, pulling herself up onto it.

"Stay with me, Doctor," Susan demanded, shuffling across to the cabinets. She opened the first sliding door and reached inside. "I won't let you die on me. Have you got that?"

Teklar winced. "I hear you."

"Now, tell me, what am I looking at here? I don't know how to read Gunosien." Susan ran one finger over the tiny vials, while finding a small stream injector with the other. It was like the same device Iarinos had dosed her with before her surgery.

"There should be a blue container," the doctor told her.

Susan found it and yanked it from the cabinet. "You're sure?"

"Yes."

"What about—"

"Green container, with a red band around it," Teklar shot back.

Susan grabbed both vials, a pack of gauze, bandages, and a handheld scanner. She flung all the supplies onto the floor next to the doctor below and grasped the side of the bed. She threw herself down and fell in a heap beside her patient. Uncrumpling herself, she attached the vial of pain relief to the injector and administered it into Teklar's arm.

A hint of reprieve appeared on the Gunosien's face, and she mouthed the words 'thank you' to her. Susan so desperately wanted to experience the same comfort, but it would have to wait. She prepared for the rest of the procedure, but just as she was about to administer the blood-thickening agent, a blast wailed outside the door.

Susan froze, and the doctor stared at her. Neither of the women moved.

Another blast rang out, and Susan put a calming hand on her patient, injecting her again and wrapping her wound. She left her by herself for a moment and crawled to the edge of the bed to see what was happening.

In the lobby, the Xanian soldiers formed a line from the entrance and fought off unknown resistance at the top of the staircase.

Teklar groaned, and Susan returned to her side. The Gunosien convulsed, and blood spurted from her mouth. Susan injected her with another dose of the blood-thickening agent and examined the reading on her scanner. Even in a different language, it was obvious what the device were telling her.

The gunfire neared, and a Xanian backed up into the clinic against the wall. The being looked down at the pair, and its insectoid eyes bulged. Quick to move, it aimed its gun at them and prepared to fire.

TWENTY-SIX

The Xanian stared down at Susan just as she would have at a bug when she was a child playing in her backyard sandpit. The alien must have wondered what kind of species she was and what she was doing on Gunos. But his curiosity only went so far as his finger slowly moved toward the trigger of his gun.

Teklar groaned behind them, and the soldier flinched, training his rifle on her instead.

Susan took her chance and grabbed the injector and slammed it into the foot of the Xanian with the largest dose she could give him. The alien froze and screeched so loud she had to cover her ears. His limbs stiffened, but his rifle remained on target. Susan picked up the scanner next to her and grasped it in her palm. She swept it at his legs, and he tumbled to the floor, smashing his head against the edge of the bed. The gun clattered from his hands and dropped between the two women.

Susan edged to his side and looked into the fascinating insectoid eyes of the creature, finding her skewed reflection inside them. She glanced out at the lobby, where his compatriots continued to attack whoever had dared to fight back against them.

Susan crawled over to Teklar. "We have to get out of here, Doctor."

But the woman didn't respond.

Susan put her hand on her wrist and retrieved the scanner to take her readings.

But there was no heart rate. No pulse.

She dropped her head and threw the handheld device into the wall. "Dammit!"

Before she could mourn her fellow physician, more footsteps moved in her direction from the lobby. She peeked out to find two more Xanians backing toward the alcove-shaped entrance to take cover.

Susan didn't like the idea of shooting someone in the back, but whoever they were, they were hostile to Gunos. Millions had already likely perished at their hand. She did a quick inspection of the Xanian energy weapon and found the trigger in an awkward position up the barrel, no doubt exactly where it needed to be for the bug-like appendages of the insectoid species. She propped herself on her front and aimed at the nearest of the incoming targets.

Then she fired.

The beam blasted from the barrel of the rifle and dropped the Xanian to the floor.

Its comrade checked behind him, flinching at the strike, and did a double-take ahead, caught between a rock and a hard place. Susan took aim again, but before she could nail him with her rifle, someone in the lobby got the shot in before her.

A Gunosien, joined by other security guards and hospital staff who had taken up the cause against their invaders, waved forward toward the entrance of the hospital.

More of the Xanian soldiers streamed from the landing pad and went on a counterattack of their own. Both parties filled the lobby with weapon fire, while Susan remained in her position and peppered potshots at the incoming aliens. Unfortunately, the Gunosiens were out of their element, and the Xanians, with greater numbers, pushed them farther back into the building. Susan tried to get off more covering fire, but the Xanians set their sights on her, and she got quickly pinned down, too.

"How many of these guys do I have to take out?" she muttered, rubbing her barely functional legs.

The Xanians filled the lobby, and the cries from the Gunosiens called out as they went down one by one. Susan realized she'd be the next one on the chopping block and looked around the small confines for an emergency exit. Nothing presented itself. That was until she found a panel on the wall. She dragged herself to it and reached up, waving her hand in front of it.

A medical tube, not dissimilar to the one she'd been placed in for surgery, slid from a slot in the wall.

The footsteps of the Xanians rapidly neared.

What choice do I have?

She climbed up, using what was left of the strength in her upper arms, and jumped in, closing the lid over the top of her. Outside in the alcove, the footsteps of the Xanians scratched against the floor with their gangly legs. She breathed in and out, preparing for the inevitable.

Susan gripped the rifle that much tighter, and the latch to the tube clicked. The lid opened, and the grotesque features of the pair of Xanians appeared above her.

The soldiers lurched backward but kept their fingers clasped around their weapons.

"Surprise!" Susan fired her rifle at the closest one, and he launched across the clinic into the row of cabinets, smashing the doors and sending the supplies inside it onto the floor.

Its comrade, quick to action, leaped at her and knocked the gun from her grip. One of his hands went for her throat and the other for his own weapon.

Susan swatted it away and yanked at his other hand.

But he was strong. Much stronger than she would have guessed with his insect-like limbs.

The two tussled, and both flew from the medical tube onto the floor.

Susan fell on top of the Xanian, and he squealed. She put all her bodyweight on him and punched his face over and over again.

But the soldier's strength continued to surprise her, and he flipped her over, taking the position of power away. He coiled his long legs around her lower body and barreled his fist into her head.

She blocked the repeated punches as best she could, but she couldn't break free. Then he got a good one in, hitting her cheekbone flush and putting a crack through it.

Susan cried out, and he stopped for the tiniest of moments, as if to gloat. Pushing the pain aside, she reached behind her for the scanner and swatted it in his face.

He went tumbling off her, and she shuffled backward for her gun. She lunged for the rifle and turned.

But the Xanian beat her to it, reaching for his own weapon and aiming it straight at her.

Then came the blast.

Susan closed her eyes.

Then nothing.

I'm not dead?

She reopened her eyes to find the Xanian on the floor with a bullet hole in its back slumped in front of her.

At the door, Jason Cassidy and Aly Rycroft stood with their rifles raised in the air.

TWENTY-SEVEN

Planet Zero

The farther the expedition marched through the remains of the ruins, the more warped the structure of the building became. While the alloy used by the Kalceni was strong, after so many millennia, with the exterior stress compounding against it, it was only a matter of time before it crumbled away.

"Lucky we didn't come here another million years later," Javier quipped, checking the readings on his handheld scanner.

Onlor continued on, as if he hadn't heard him. He stopped at a four-way junction at the end of the corridor and peered down each walkway. To that point, they'd found similar scenes to the one on the observation level. It reminded Javier of the ruins of Pompeii, where the ancient Romans who were excavated appeared to be going about their everyday life just as the apocalypse struck.

"Which way, Professor?" Onlor asked.

Javier checked his scanner, finding smaller rooms, similar to the offices on the levels above. But ahead, something different revealed itself. "I'm picking up a larger space in that direction."

The Company leader brushed past him, and everyone else followed. The floor at its entry had mostly collapsed, but the edges were still intact. Onlor went first and did it with ease. Javier, being much older and more careful, tiptoed over it, holding on to a beam from the crumpled wall. Once he was in the clear on the other side, he did his best to catch up to Onlor, who was already examining the large circular space with his flashlight.

Surrounding them on every wall were bookcases as tall as the ceiling, filled with thousands, if not tens of thousands of texts. Javier walked over to the nearest collection of books and studied the spines. They were all in the same Kalceni language he'd deciphered from his time aboard the weapon ship at Psi-Aion. He picked one out at random and opened it, but just as he was about to turn a page, the entire book deteriorated in his hands and dropped to the floor in a pile of dust.

Onlor approached and yanked out the one next to it. It too disintegrated. He then pressed on the rest of the books on the shelf, and they broke apart like powder. "The secrets of the Kalceni..."

Javier rubbed the remnants of his text between his fingers. "It would seem the passage of time was a lot kinder to the bones of the Kalceni than it was their records."

At the archway, the other members of the expedition made their way over the threshold. They waved their flashlights around, lighting up the entire library. Javier strolled to the center and took in its almost Gothic-like brilliance. While it was just as dark as any other Kalceni space he'd walked into, there was something different about the library. All he'd known of the species was its destructive powers. The fact that there was a wisdom behind it was both reassuring and scary at the same time.

He stopped, nearly stumbling on an obstruction beneath his feet. He aimed his flashlight downward to find a series of huge patterns etched on the cold black floor. At such a close proximity to them, they didn't appear to make any sense, so he edged backward, until the lines and circles of the entire picture revealed themselves to him. "The star chart..."

Onlor hurried to his side. "You've found something?"

"This is same navigational makeup of the region I discovered in the Kalceni base's computer." Javier pointed at the largest circle represented before them. "Planet Zero."

"It's slightly raised."

"No wonder I nearly fell over it."

Onlor put his foot on it, and the circle lowered into the floor. He looked at Javier and shrugged. But then a light activated on the ceiling above their heads. The pair stepped backward, and a beam burst forth from it. At the heart of the library, a semi-transparent figure materialized.

Onlor's jaw dropped. "A hologram?"

Javier nodded at the female image before them. But it wasn't the fact they'd discovered the hologram that surprised him the most. It was the species it represented.

Onlor twigged as well. "She's Retebu?"

Javier wondered if he'd finally pieced it together. "No, she's not."

The female hologram raised her eyebrows at him, showing signs that it comprehended them and her surroundings.

"What are you talking about, Professor?" Onlor asked. "She's like the one you call Kione—a Retebu."

"Similar..." Javier walked around the hologram and returned to the Ulvekan's side. "The Kalceni bodies upstairs were the first physical examples of their race I've ever come across."

"Of course, because they used other races as hosts."

"Right. When I did a scan on the remains, I picked up something a little odd." He activated his scanner and showed Onlor a reading he'd taken of the skeletons on the observation level. "The Kalceni and Retebu aren't as dissimilar as we thought. Their DNA is remarkably alike but slightly different at the same time."

"Which means what exactly?"

"I theorize the Kalceni and the Retebu must have

evolved on the same world and were once the same species."

Onlor blinked a few times, glancing across at the hologram.

"You are correct," she finally said.

The pair turned to her as she spoke to them in a very calm and almost lyrical tone. All the other members of the expedition joined them and surrounded the hologram.

"So, the two oldest races of the galaxy were actually one?" Onlor asked her.

"Once upon a time," the hologram continued. "However, there was a schism. An ideological struggle took place on the Retebu world. War ensued, resulting in the Kalceni's need to find another home."

"Planet Zero." Javier nodded. "That's why you designated it as Zero, because the Retebu world was Planet One."

"That is correct."

Onlor moved closer to her. "Why the difference in DNA?"

"Because the planet we're standing on was the most habitable world the Kalceni could find. And while it was similar to Planet One, it was initially quite inhospitable to our species. The scientists of our day had no choice but to alter themselves at a genetic level to survive."

"Astounding." Onlor shook his head. "You're like a backup mechanism, aren't you? These books around us, the knowledge in them, is in you, isn't it?"

The hologram nodded. "All the knowledge from this world remains inside me. As long as the spire atop this building is functioning, drawing in the solar energy of this star system, I will forever function."

"Fantastic!"

The echo of the expedition leader's excitement rang out around the library, and Javier warily rounded the hologram.

Onlor crossed his arms as if he were an old-time cop about to begin an interrogation. "Then you can tell us of the final conflict between the Retebu and Kalceni?"

"No, she can't." Javier stopped on the other side of her and stared through the transparent projection at Onlor. "Think about it. That conflict was fought with the power of Retebu spheres. What you see around us are the results from an earlier feud, waged with more conventional weapons of the day. The Kalceni must have survived this particular war and settled somewhere else before the period in history we're more familiar with."

The hologram put out her hand, and a battle taking place over Planet Zero appeared. Several vessels fired upon each other with two distinctly unique designs. "The Retebu laid waste to this world." The images altered to a vision of cities crumbling to the ground, and then to the Kalceni ships moving away from orbit. "You are correct. The Kalceni had no choice but to evacuate Planet Zero."

"And that's the limit of your knowledge, isn't it?" Javier said.

The hologram nodded. "You are the first beings to set foot upon this world since the last of the Kalceni fled."

Onlor frowned.

"That's not to say she doesn't hold a plethora of information." Javier returned to his side. "She should be able to tell us more about the Kalceni, and the Retebu as well."

"You claim the Kalceni evacuated their world," the Ulvekan said to hologram. "They did so in ships. Did they have a Plan B, just in case they weren't successful?"

Javier turned to the projection, who raised her eyebrows at the pair. "You speak of the Eternal Plan?"

"The Eternal Plan?" Onlor's glum expression vanished, and a smile appeared. "Tell me more."

TWENTY-EIGHT

Cargo Ship Argo

Kevin examined Susan's body with his medical scanner and shook his head at the doctor lying on the bed inside his infirmary.

"This is amazing," he said. "They really gave you back your legs, didn't they?"

She winced from the bruises she'd been given from her hand-to-hand combat with the Xanians. Even craning her neck made her healed jaw throb in agony. Before she could ask for any more pain relief, a familiar figure stepped through the door with a smile as large as life.

"Jason Cassidy." Susan did her best to return his happiness.

"I knew we'd meet again, but I didn't expect it'd be under these circumstances." He stopped by her bedside. "Come to think of it, with all the whacky stuff that's been occurring lately, I probably should've foreseen this happening at some point."

"Have we left Gunos?" she asked.

He grabbed the spare chair on the other side of the bed and sat, doing his best to stay out of Kevin's way as he continued to do his tests. "We cleared the planet's orbit and got back to the gateway unscathed. We're now using the network to head back to Earth."

"What about Doctor Iarinos and the others?"

"They declined my offer to come with us, after we rescued them from the Xanians. They said there was work for them to do on Gunos."

Susan sighed. "What do you think will happen to them?"

"I don't like their chances. It appears their invaders took them by surprise. Organizing a resistance against them will be difficult."

"Hopefully, the Alliance can put a fleet together to intervene."

Jason darted his eyes sideways. "I wouldn't count on it."

Susan went to say something, but Kevin stopped between them and injected her with more pain relief. Her limbs turned to jelly, and her head became woozy. "That's some potent stuff. What exactly did you give me?"

Kevin winked at her. "Get some sleep."

He walked off, and Susan gazed out at Jason as everything around her started spinning. She grabbed him by the cuff of his jacket and pulled him in closer. "Thank you for rescuing me."

He put a hand on her shoulder. "We'll chat when you wake up."

Susan's eyelids slowly closed, and she fell into a much-sought slumber.

Aly was sitting at the helm when Jason arrived on the bridge while Althaus stood over the operations station, propping himself up awkwardly with his crutches. He prodded at the controls furiously, his brow creasing further with every push.

"Where are we at, Aly?" Jason asked.

"We're approaching the end of the trans-space corridor." She pointed to the star chart on the monitor in front of her revealing the regional gateway network, which looked like a splattered plate of spaghetti. "Once we're clear, we'll have to transit to the next one."

"How long until we arrive at Mirin's drop-off point?"

"Half a day."

Jason frowned.

Aly mirrored the expression. "You're going to miss her."

He leaned against the console and crossed his arms. "Aren't you?"

"Yeah, I suppose I am. Maybe, when this is all over, we could—"

Althaus's grunts stopped her mid-sentence.

Jason glared at him. "What the hell are you doing over there?"

"Ask your girlfriend," he fired back.

Aly rolled her eyes. "Ever since we took the *Argo* through Gunos' atmosphere, we've been having some intermittent issues with the ship's systems. The scanners have been playing up, but there's nothing physically wrong with any of the components. Althaus is checking out the software."

"A bit out of your depth, Uncle?" Jason jested.

Althaus scowled, throwing his crutches to the deck and planting himself in the chair.

"While I'd love to stay and continue watching our resident gorilla kick in his cage, I might leave you to it." Jason kissed her on the forehead and made his way through the door, down the elevator to his quarters.

He sprawled out on his bed and put his head in his hands. He wanted to sleep so badly, unable to remember the last time he'd got a quick kip. But he refused to be a lazy captain. He couldn't rest while his crew were hard at work getting them home. He stood back up and opened his closet to find a fresh pair of clothes. Ones that didn't smell of dried blood from the insects they'd had to carve through to rescue Doctor Tai.

Jason yanked a new jacket from the coat hanger, and his guitar fell onto his feet. He picked it up and twanged at a few of the strings, creating an awful tune. With a smile, he took the guitar with him and left his quarters.

Mirin laid out her rokei mat on the deck of the *Julieanne* and sat, crossing one leg over the other. She placed her hands together and breathed in and out, achieving the rhythm she desired. Unfortunately, every time she inhaled, the stench of the humans entered her lungs. No matter what she'd done to filter the odor, it still lingered in the air.

All her muscles relaxed, and she let her limbs go as elastic as possible. The worries of the day disappeared, and her mind emptied of all the internal voices inside it. It might have been the most at peace she'd felt since arriving.

Then a clang sounded somewhere in the outside world, and a series of footsteps pounded against the deck, echoing around her.

"Mirin, are you in here?" someone called out.

She snapped her eyes open, and Jason Cassidy appeared through the side airlock of the small craft, with an unusual stringed instrument in his hand.

"I'm so sorry." Jason's face reddened, and he took a step backward. "I didn't mean to—"

"It's okay." She stood, and everything from the day came pouring back to her.

"I can return later. I'll show you this another—"

"Please." She folded up her rokei and placed it under her arm. "I can meditate whenever I want. There's only so much time left that I'll be able to listen to this guitar of yours."

Jason pulled the instrument closer to him. But before he could twang a string, his attention wavered, and he peered beyond Mirin. She followed his gaze to the viewport where their trans-space corridor had dissipated and normal space appeared.

"We're coming out of the gateway," Jason said. "It won't be long until we arrive at your drop-off point."

Mirin's original plan had gone up in smoke because of the *Argo's* crew's propensity to get themselves into trouble. Time was of the essence, and the longer she waited, the less likely she'd be able to accomplish her mission.

Turning away from him for a moment, she took out the injector from her pocket and slid it down the cuff of her shirt. She spun back around and approached him. "Play me something. Please."

Jason put the strap of the guitar over his shoulders and strummed some strings. The sound wasn't unlike the turaja instrument native to her home world, which used similar vibrations in a large wooden box to produce acoustic music.

He closed his eyes and broke out into a melody. The tune was completely foreign to her, but it was quite soothing. And sad.

Mirin frowned and took her chance, lunging at the human and injecting him in his arm.

Jason's eyes burst open, and he looked at her with his mouth agape. He tried to speak, but no words came out. He fell, and she caught him before he could slam to the deck. With a deft hand, she removed the guitar from around his neck and strapped him into a seat in the rear compartment.

TWENTY-NINE

"I think you've got it."

Aly's father stood behind her as she completed routing the feed from the ship's communications antenna via the gateway comm network.

Aly had wondered for a while if it was possible to use the Alliance tech to expand their ability to pick up commonwealth news channels and feed them directly to the *Argo*. So far, she'd had no luck, but with the appearance of a blurred image on the rec room's wall monitor, she finally thought she might be onto something.

Just as it started taking shape, however, the screen went blank. Aly placed her hands on her hips, and her dad peered over her shoulder at the exposed panel.

"Perhaps if you—"

"Who's the engineer here?" she shot back at him with a cheeky grin.

Her father put his hands up in surrender and stepped back, allowing her to try again. With a minor adjustment to the connection, the monitor sprang to life.

A news anchor appeared behind a desk somewhere in one of Earth's studios. The transmission was choppy but watchable.

"Nice work," her dad commended her.

Aly packed her tools away on the ping-pong table, and the pair turned to Althaus stepping into the rec room.

"You got it working?" he said, incredulously.

Aly dialed up the volume, and the anchor's voice rose.

"Word continues to come out of the Alliance of reports of hostility spreading throughout the member worlds. Old rivalries have been renewed, and the planets seceding from the intergalactic community mount every day."

The camera panned out, and the singular talking head became two. The anchor swiveled in his chair to the woman next to him. *"With me this evening is foreign correspondent Kathleen Wise, who joins me for the first time since returning from the Alliance. I hope you had a pleasant trip through the gateway."*

She nodded. *"Thank you for having me on."*

"Let's get to the matter at hand. Everyone out there in the commonwealth wants to know what's happening beyond the gateway."

"Unfortunately, it's a very complex question," she said. *"But what we're effectively seeing is a collapse of an idea. In my time reporting on matters in the Alliance, I've come to see it as a galactic version of Ancient Rome. Rome was a small city state which grew to take over a*

sizeable part of the world through military conquest, expanding their culture and assimilating the surrounding lands. The Alliance did this much more democratically, without the use of slavery and the bread and circuses of the Roman civilization. A fundamental ideal of the Alliance is that the whole is greater than the sum. That greatness is achieved via teamwork."

"So, what's changed?" the anchor asked.

"We have to go back a long way to dig up the seeds of discontent, but the current predicament began with Cuneris' secession," she continued. *"No one in the entire history of the Alliance had ever done what they did. What made it even more shocking is that Cuneris was a founding member."*

The anchor narrowed his eyes. *"What prompted it?"*

"This stems from the Kalceni incident. The weapon ship which carved its way through the Alliance was akin to the sack of Rome. Even though the Alliance won the battle, it showed they were no longer invincible. Resources became scarce for the first time in centuries, supplies lines fell, and military aid was limited. A lot of planets struggled with the compromises which had to be made. The Cunerians believe they can do it better on their own. Other planets have come to the same conclusion. What's happening is mini alliances are being formed and old conflicts which once existed over disputes of territory are coming to the fore. Fighting has broken out, and the current government is powerless to stop it. They just don't have the resources or manpower since the Kalceni attack."

"All Empires end, don't they?"

"That's true. But while I describe the Alliance as a modern-day Rome, its radically different in terms of what it stands for. The Alliance is a worthwhile ideal. I still hold out hope that cooler heads will prevail, because if they don't the outcome could be catastrophic."

The anchor frowned. *"And where do you see the commonwealth's position on this?"*

"President Rollo has been reticent to say much to this point." Wise steepled her fingers on the desk. *"Apart from requesting all commonwealth nationals return from the other side of the gateway, she's played her cards close to her chest. We've only just joined the Alliance, so we won't rock the boat. Even if we did, we can't expect our voice to amount to much."*

"I wonder where Jason is." Aly activated her commband. "Aly to Jason." She eyed the two men beside her at the lack of response. "Do you read?"

Again, he didn't reply.

"When did you see him last?" her dad asked.

"Before we did our transfer at the gateway," she said. "Have either of you seen him since?"

Both shook their heads.

"He's probably turned his commband off. I hope he hasn't crawled into the bottom of another bottle." She looked knowingly at her father. "I'll go find him."

Aly left the rec room and searched everywhere on A Deck, including the infirmary, wondering if he might be with Tai. All she found were the lights off and the doctor fast asleep on her bed. Aly continued on to B

Deck, coming across much of the same emptiness. There was at least some comfort in the fact he wasn't in the bathroom vomiting up his stomach.

Then she twigged to his most predictable habits when he wanted to be alone. She hopped back on the elevator and shot down to the cargo bay. "Jason?" her voice echoed around the empty hold. "Are you here?"

She stepped toward the airlock of the *Julieanne*, and her commband beeped. "Yes, what is it?"

"Have you found him?" her father asked.

"Not yet. I think he's in the *Julieanne*. It's the only place he can be."

"What about Mirin?"

"What do you mean?"

"When I went to the bridge to check on the helm, the systems station was showing a malfunction in Mirin's quarters. Seems she's been fiddling with the environmental filters. I tried to find her in her quarters, but she wasn't in there either."

"She's probably in the *Julieanne* with Jason. I'll let you know in a second." Aly stopped at the airlock, finding it sealed in place, and peered through small viewport. Where the interior of the transport should have been was replaced with the swirling colors of transspace.

A lump formed in her throat, and she pulled the commband closer to her face. "Uh, Dad, we have a problem."

THIRTY

Brielaro

Javier sat at the massive circular table of the Company ship's briefing room, while around him the other members of the expedition chatted away in small groups. It was the first time since the start of the mission that everyone was in the same room, and even though he was used to large gatherings, all the egos were making the outer walls feel as if they were caving in on him.

Onlor finally arrived, and the conversation evaporated. There was a determination in his stride. To that point he'd been quite hands-off, but since their visit to the world below he'd well and truly taken the reins. He took up his place at the head of the table on the opposite side to Javier and activated the holographic projector, bathing the room in images from their dig on the surface of Planet Zero.

The meeting was very dry, even for Javier. Onlor went around the table to each team leader who voiced their findings and opinions on their specific fields in regard to the ruins of Planet Zero. Onlor then reached Javier, who almost flinched at his name being called out.

"Professor, how are we looking confirming the hologram's claims that the Retebu and the Kalceni are in fact a related species?"

Javier stood, and every eyeball in the room shifted toward him. "I've liaised with Specialist Utombra who's been analyzing the computer archives. She's concluded the records are accurate."

"There's no sign of malfunction?" Onlor asked.

"No. With the constant stream of power from the solar spire, there's been no interruption. It's remained in perfect working order for all these years."

"You also had Doctor Pov'Latan examining the skeletal remains?"

Javier nodded. "He's examined the DNA of the Kalceni we discovered on Planet Zero and cross-checked it with Kione's DNA, which we have on record. The similarities are as the hologram claims. They were once one species, only slightly removed due to genetic engineering and potentially some environmental changes."

Onlor continued with his questioning and moved on to the rest of the scientists. Once he reached the other side of the table, everyone breathed out a sigh of relief and murmurs again started rumbling. The Ulvekan stood and put his hand up to restore some order, and silence again filled the briefing room.

"Today has been a spectacular day for the Alliance,"

he said. "While we're all concerned about what's happening back home, I think we can all be proud of what we've achieved here. Examining the data alone will keep us busy for years to come. Hopefully our discoveries will lead to a solution should the Kalceni ever pose a threat to us again. It's because of that reason I'd like our resources to shift toward the study of what the hologram has described as the Eternal Plan."

Javier, though fatigued, raised his brow. Onlor's eyes gleamed just as much as they had when he'd discovered the Kalceni library.

Javier put up his hand as if he were a schoolboy.

Onlor pointed to him from across the table. "Yes, Professor?"

"There's the distinct possibility we'll discover more of the ancient Kalceni civilization on the surface," he said. "If I may ask, what makes the Eternal Plan such a priority?"

Onlor stared at him, stone-faced. "If it wasn't for the Eternal Plan, the Kalceni would've been extinct millions of years ago. If it wasn't for the Eternal Plan, the Kalceni never would've outlived the Retebu. If it wasn't for the Eternal Plan, the Kalceni never would've attacked the Alliance. As far as I'm concerned, their ability at quasi-immortality is as much a weapon as the spheres. If not more so. I want to be ready if we or future generations have to face them again. And as the famed researcher you are, I'd imagine you can appreciate the scientific curiosity of the unknown this represents."

Javier smiled wryly. "The unknown has been my friend for a very long time. It's also been something I've learned to be wary of."

Onlor glared at him in a way he'd never seen before. While he was a man of few emotions, rarely did he ever show displeasure. "I couldn't agree more. Why do you think I brought with me some of the best minds the galaxy has to offer?"

The scientists around the table nodded at each other with the sufficient stroking of their ego achieved.

"From this moment forward," Onlor continued, "I want you to focus all your efforts on studying the Eternal Plan. That means finding everything you can in the library's computers. I don't want to leave his place without knowing what the Kalceni knew."

Everyone stood from their chairs and filed out of the briefing room. Javier lingered behind, and he and Onlor looked at each other across the table. They were like two prize fighters before a bout. The Company leader's eyes began to go bloodshot and quiver ever so slightly. He finally turned and departed, leaving Javier alone in the empty room.

Out in the corridor, Doctor Unaporvan stopped him while some of the other scientists watched on. "You seem agitated, Professor," he whispered.

"And here I thought I was keeping myself in check." Javier shook his head. "Don't worry, I'm just a little concerned. I'll be okay."

The two parted ways, and Javier went to the bridge, where he found the ship's primary communications officer at his station. As was usual with the time of the day, there were few others around, while the *Brielaro* remained in orbit of Planet Zero.

"Good evening, Kranlar," Javier said.

"Professor." He glanced at him as he approached.

"You know what I came here to ask, don't you?"

A smile appeared on the alien's youthful face. "You want to know if your message reached its destination?"

"Well...?"

"Not only has it been received. But a reply recently came through."

"Excellent."

Kranlar put his hands on the console. "Would you like me to bring the message up?"

"Uh." Javier scanned the bridge. "Maybe I'll take it in my quarters. Nothing personal, Kranlar, but sometimes—"

"I get it, Professor. Don't worry, I understand the value of privacy. When you go to your quarters, it'll be waiting for you to access on your computer."

Javier let the junior Ulvekan return to his duties, and he made his way to his quarters. Just as promised, there on the computer was the stored message. He turned the lights on and took a seat, waving his hand over the holographic projection. A familiar face in the form of a Krostesian appeared in front of him.

"Hello, Professor," the dour Jushlan Faranar greeted him. It was the same expression his friend sported when they'd worked together on the construction of Earth's trans-space gateway. Javier wasn't sure if it was a trait of

his species or a man who, at two hundred and fifty years old, had got tired of smiling. *"I was pleased to hear from you, though dismayed it's been so long since our work on your home world."*

Javier felt ashamed that he hadn't kept in contact with him, but his life had taken a few twists and turns since his time on the project.

"I've looked into your queries through some of my connections and I've got some news you'll be interested in."

Javier leaned in closer, toward the hologram.

"It would seem that Garin Onlor, the leader of your expedition, is in fact no longer employed as an officer of the Company," Faranar said. *"Twelve months ago, he was given his marching orders. From what I can tell, however, he had a lot of contacts in the Company and managed to procure himself a vessel with his previous accreditations. Once upon a time it would have been impossible, but with everything going on at the moment in the Alliance, it doesn't surprise me in the least that something of this nature has fallen through the cracks. You were duped, my friend. I hope you can do something with the information I've given you. Stay safe out there."*

THIRTY-ONE

Transport Pod Julieanne

Jason's eyelids slowly opened, and the familiar weathered brown of the *Julieanne's* ceiling filled his vision. The deck beneath reverberated, and he quickly realized it meant one thing—the pod was in motion.

He tried to get up, but something stopped him from moving his arms from behind his back. "What the hell!"

Jason glanced over his shoulder and flipped himself onto his front, to find both hands and ankles restrained with a pair of strong manacles. He nudged himself over onto his back again and shifted himself so he could see the forward section of the pod. Whatever had happened, he was traveling through trans-space. And by the pair of feet planted on the floor on the other side of the chair, there was someone at the controls.

"What's going on here?" he demanded.

The seat swiveled ever so slightly, and Mirin revealed herself. Jason widened his eyes at her and the guitar leaning against the console.

"You attacked me?" he said, attempting to piece everything together that happened to him before blacking out.

"I'm sorry," she told him. "What I injected you with has the propensity to give you slight memory loss. It should return to you shortly."

Jason recalled coming down to the cargo bay to find Mirin meditating on her lonesome aboard the *Julieanne*. "What the hell did you inject me with?"

"It was just a mild sedative," she reassured him. "Though I've never seen someone as unconscious as you before. You were the first human I've used it on, so there were bound to be some surprises."

Jason struggled with his restraints. "If you're so sorry for drugging me, why did you do it?"

Mirin checked the helm monitors. "It had to be done."

"That's not an answer. Where's the *Argo*? If you've harmed my crew, I'll—"

"Nothing has happened to your ship, and no one was harmed. They're likely still on course for Earth. As to why I'm doing this, that's not for me to say. At least not yet."

Jason crawled closer to her as best he could hog-tied with his restraints. "You know they'll come looking for me. Tell me what's going on."

Mirin refocused her attention on the viewport.

"You're in no place to demand anything, Jason. Those cuffs are made of Verusian steel, and even if you somehow break free, do you think you'd stand a chance against me?"

Jason frowned, remembering the beating she'd given the green goliath back on Myjurna Station. He didn't particularly want to be on the receiving end of her advanced fighting prowess. "You can't just kidnap me from my ship."

"I'm not kidnapping you, Jason," she said, in the same calm manner she'd had ever since he'd regained consciousness.

"You tying me up and stealing my pod is abduction, no matter what way you look at it. If you wanted the *Julieanne*, you could have just taken it. You didn't have to bring me along for the ride."

She shook her head. "I have no interest in your pod. It's an antiquated mode of transport. I'm amazed your species left your world in these fragile crafts."

Jason scowled. But he couldn't deny the construction techniques used by the races of the Alliance were much different to those back home in the commonwealth. To them the *Julieanne* would have seemed like a horse and cart compared to their own technology.

"Okay, so, you want me? Why?" he asked. "Are you putting me up for ransom or something? Believe me, there's more important people out in the galaxy. Like literally anyone."

"I have no interest in making money from you." Mirin made a slight change to the pod's equilibrium, ensuring it was stable inside the trans-space corridor. "You're a lot more important than all the riches of the galaxy put together."

"Important to who?" Jason scoffed.

She didn't reply, and he pulled hard against his restraints, flipping himself back over.

"Jason, please, save your strength," she said.

"Save my strength? For what?"

Cargo Ship Argo

"Can you see that?"

Althaus pointed at the monitor on the operations station while Aly looked over his shoulder, examining the hazy images on the ship's scanners.

"Can you clean that up any more?" she asked.

Althaus glared at her. "Be thankful it's this clear. Whatever Mirin did wreaked havoc with our systems."

Aly put an apologetic hand on his arm. "So, going by this, when we came out of that last gateway, the *Julieanne* detached and shot through another gateway to..."

"Somewhere."

"How could the transport pod have left the ship without setting off the airlock sensors?" She crossed her arms. "None of the logs are coming up with anything."

"If Mirin's been playing with the scanners and her environmental controls, she's probably had her hands in the cargo bay systems, too."

Aly walked to the captain's chair and spun the

empty seat around. The dread in her stomach, which had festered ever since discovering Jason was missing, continued to churn. "Any ideas how we might find which gateway they took?"

Althaus swiveled in his chair. "Not with the scanner data we have. There were six gateways at that hub. All we can be certain of is that they didn't travel through this one.

"So, there's five options." Aly bit her bottom lip. "He could be anywhere by now."

Althaus nodded.

"*Kevin to bridge,*" her dad's voice filtered over the speakers.

Althaus pressed in the intercom.

"Go ahead," Aly said.

"*Can you come down to the infirmary, please?*"

Her and Althaus looked at one another, noticing the urgency in his tone. They both hurried through the hatchway, down the corridor, and into the ship's medical section. Inside, Aly's dad stood over the medical console with Doctor Tai beside him on a set of crutches similar to Althaus's.

"What have you found?" Aly asked.

He directed her attention to the monitor. "I've scanned her quarters from top to bottom, and it seems we've discovered Mirin's DNA sequence from a single hair."

She stared at the double helix hypnotically twisting around in front of her. "Okay, what does it tell us?"

Her father glanced at Tai, who still looked quite

frazzled since Gunos, but there was now some color in her face that wasn't there before.

"I've seen this sequence before," the doctor said. "When I was attempting to find a cure for Jung's Disease, I catalogued DNA from all kinds of different species throughout the Alliance and beyond, to see if it might be the key to coming up with a solution."

"You're telling us you can recognize a species by looking at its DNA?" Althaus asked.

"It's just another kind of language. There's always a pattern."

"So what race is Mirin?" Aly said.

"Plauvian."

"Never heard of them."

"I doubt you would have." Tai winced, shifting some of her weight on her crutches. "Their world isn't actually a member of the Alliance. They're an independent planet located beyond the Alliance's farthest border. While they have their own gateway, they keep very much to themselves."

"What could a race who keeps to themselves want with Jason?"

Tai shook her head. "I couldn't say."

Aly turned to her father. "Can you bring up the gateway network directory?"

He pushed in a series of keys, and the double helix disappeared, replaced with something she could more easily decipher. She ran her finger over the monitor and traced back their course to the hub.

"So, if we go back, we can take this gateway, which

will lead to here. That gateway should then lead us all the way to Plauvia." Aly sighed. "You weren't kidding when you said they were *beyond* the Alliance border, were you?"

THIRTY-TWO

Transport Pod Julieanne

Jason stretched out in his seat in the rear compartment, which Mirin had so generously allowed him to sit in. He was still restrained, but it was a damn sight more comfortable than being on the deck. He'd finally given up trying to break free. Mirin was right. There was no way he could go toe to toe with her, no matter how much bigger than her he was. He figured he'd have to bide his time for an opportunity to present itself.

The trans-space corridor around them dispersed, and Jason craned his neck so he could get the best vantage point from his position in the back of the *Julieanne*. Mirin, who had said little since he'd regained consciousness, danced her fingers over the console and pushed the transport pod away from the gateway exit.

Ahead, the stars greeted them, but at the heart of the viewport, one object appeared much larger than the others. As they closed in, it grew into a large yellow orb.

Jason thought he was looking at Venus for a moment, but through the white clouds, continents and sporadic seas became visible.

"Where are we, Mirin?" he asked.

She continued to close in on the planet's orbit and directed the transport pod through its upper atmosphere. "This is Plauvia."

"Plauvia?"

"My home."

The *Julieanne* juddered through the turbulence, while the heat shield glowed bright orange. The pod eventually cleared the worst of it, and the surface appeared. Though covered in mostly desert, there were quite large swathes of blue, but also some green near the edges of the land masses.

Much to Jason's dismay, Mirin turned the craft away from one of the more vibrant areas of the planet and steered them toward the heart of the desert. They dropped on a region filled with numerous rock formations and touched down, sinking ever so slightly in the soft sand.

Mirin got out of her seat. "Are you ready?"

"Depends what for?" Jason said.

"On your feet."

He stood awkwardly, and she pressed a button on a remote device in the palm of her hand. The restraints on his ankles dropped to the deck, and he kicked them away. Mirin pointed to the airlock, and Jason ducked through it and out into the open.

The warm sun beat down on him, and he lowered

his head to prevent the annoying glare. Around him, the sands were so vast they reached the horizon, and the rock formations so huge they almost blocked out the sun. "This is a hell of a place you've brought me to, Mirin. Unless there's some kind of resort here serving heavy liquor, I think I'd like to go home now."

She said nothing to his juvenile humor, instead motioning him ahead through the rocks. They marched their way up a sizeable dune and stopped at its edge. Beyond their position a structure revealed itself from the sands, while people went about their business around it.

A trio broke off and headed toward them. All three were of the same species as Mirin, but the one at the center was much older than the two beside him. He had long gray hair, tied into a ponytail, which ran halfway down his back. They stopped in front of Jason and Mirin, and the eldest looked Jason up and down.

"You've done well, Mirin," he said to her in a deep, raspy voice.

She bowed to him and stepped backward, allowing him to move closer to Jason. "You must be Jason Cassidy."

Jason glanced at the four-pointed star pendant gleaming in the sun around the man's neck, nestled on his ceremonial maroon robes, identical to the symbols he'd seen on Mascoros Prime and Tadrosia. "And you must be a follower of the Firstborns."

The man smiled and held up the pendant. "You are wise, Jason."

"It's not often I get accused of that."

"Wisdom comes in many forms. It can be learned. It can be bestowed. Or you are born with it."

Jason glanced at the Plauvians around him and narrowed his eyes at the old alien. "Why am I here?"

The man let go of his pendant and motioned down the dune. "Please, come with me."

Cargo Ship Argo

"We're approaching the interchange hub."

Kevin activated the thrusters and timed them perfectly, allowing the cargo ship to coast from the gateway exit. He breathed a sigh of relief as the more familiar stars of normal space emerged. As much as he loved traveling at the breakneck speed the gateways afforded them, there was something comforting about the twinkling lights of the heavens he'd come to know and love.

His daughter approached from the systems station where she'd been conferring with Althaus and checked his monitors. "Set a course for the next gateway."

He did so immediately, adjusting the *Argo's* heading across the orbit of Luganos, home to a pair of gateways. There was an eeriness to the planet below compared to the other inhabited worlds they'd visited. Bathed in such a dull sun, Kevin could only imagine what kind of alien species had evolved on it.

Ahead, a small ring appeared and formed into the much larger gateway that would take them the rest of the way to Plauvia. Suddenly, the scanners beeped, and both he and Alyssa checked over a series of bogeys maneuvering toward the gateway to cut them off.

"I don't like the look of this," she muttered. "Althaus, what can you see?"

"I'm reading three ships," he said. "All are well-armed."

"Who isn't that we bump into lately." Alyssa's fingertips dug into the back of Kevin's chair. "Slow us down, Dad."

Kevin activated the forward thrusters, and the *Argo* came to a dead stop, opposite the trio of vessels.

Alyssa turned to the systems station. "Althaus, can you open a—"

"They're opening a commlink with us," he interrupted her.

"Good, let's hear them."

"Unknown vessel, you have entered the territory of the Jahjina Protectorate," the voice from one of the other ships filtered over the channel.

Alyssa hurried to Althaus's side and directed him to mute the channel. "Isn't this planet inhabited by the Lugani?"

"Perhaps we've entered another war zone," her father chimed in, keeping a close eye on the ships, wary of them making any sudden moves. "These Jahjina may have invaded."

"Put them back on," she said.

"You are in violation of protectorate territory. This gateway is now in the possession of the Jahjina. You must turn around immediately."

Alyssa motioned for Althaus to mute the commlink again. "Whoever they are, and whatever they're doing here, they've obviously decided to disobey Alliance law and seize it for their own control." She returned to Kevin's side. "Althaus, put me back on."

"You're on," he said.

"This is Aly Rycroft of the *Cargo Ship Argo*. We need to transit this gateway to fulfill a shipment to Plauvia. We—"

"This gateway is temporarily closed to all civilian traffic. New licensing agreements are being drawn up. If you come back at a later date—"

"I'm happy to pay the price you want now," she interrupted the Jahjina commander.

"This gateway is currently reserved for fleet movements."

"Is there any way to convince you—"

"You are to turn around immediately."

"They've cut off the commlink," Althaus said.

Alyssa stared through the viewport. "Althaus, how much of a pounding could our shields take if we went straight through them?"

He swiveled in his chair. "Let's just say, I wouldn't advise finding out."

Kevin looked into his daughter's eyes as if seeing the cogs turning in her mind. "We can go another way." He pulled up the gateway star chart on the helm, revealing the alternate route if they went back the way they'd come.

"That might be cut off, too," she said.

"Maybe, maybe not. If it isn't, we'll at least arrive in one piece." He spun his chair slightly, forcing her to look at him. "We're no good to Jason dead."

She balled her hand into a fist. "Very well. Take us about."

THIRTY-THREE

Plauvia

Jason entered the ancient Plauvian temple, which was somehow still standing, and took in his surroundings. For whatever reason it filled him with warmth. Unlike the temple of Tadrosia which was put together with whatever materials could be found, there was a sense the ruins he stood inside were built for a purpose. It truly felt like a holy site.

The cleric named Brukan invited him through the heart of the temple. It was set up similar to others he'd been to, with a lectern front and center and benches pointing toward it. But instead of the benches being constructed of wood, they were carved from the same rock which littered the region around them.

Jason made his way beyond the lectern to the wall, where a huge crystalline four-pointed star adorned it. The sunlight from the windows caused it to shimmer in every color of the rainbow. He then circled the lectern, which had a book nestled on it. He remembered the leather-bound copy on Tadrosia, which the Firstborn cleric there believed held a prophecy that Kione was their messiah who would help them break the shackles against their foes in the orbiting space stations.

Jason had concluded long before that visit that Kione was very special. Though he wasn't sure how or why until he'd destroyed the Retebu sphere on the Kalceni weapon ship. If Kione was a Guardian, as the Tadrosians claimed, they had misinterpreted the text. He wasn't delivered through time to save them, but to save the galaxy as a whole. Not a day went by when Jason didn't think about his friend, and the last time he'd seen him on Earth in the Sierra Nevada Mountains as an apparition. Or a higher form of life, as he'd put it.

Jason stared through the window into the desert surrounding the ruin. Beyond the rock formations, which likely protected the temple from some of the harsh elements, were scattered townships built with a hodgepodge of stone, wood, and metal. There were surely better places to live on Plauvia, but there seemed to be a devotion to the Firstborns that made their people do extraordinary things.

He turned around to find Mirin and Brukan standing beside the lectern. There was a thoughtfulness in their eyes. Brukan continued to examine him as he had since his arrival.

"I think it's time you got rid of those," the cleric told Mirin.

She pulled the control device from her pocket and

pressed the keypad. The restraints from Jason's hands unlatched and fell to the floor.

"You, weren't lying, were you?" Jason said to Mirin. "I'm not here to be ransomed."

Mirin shook her head.

"Please, don't blame Mirin." Brukan put a hand on the side of the stone lectern. "She was only doing the bidding of the Firstborns."

"Do you know how often I've heard you guys say that guff?" Jason clenched his fists. "Come on, spill the beans. What am I doing here?"

Brukan picked up the book and clutched it tight in his hands. "You're here, Jason, because we need your help."

"You need my help?" He laughed. "That's why you abducted me from my ship and crew?"

Mirin stepped forward. "I apologize, Jason. It wasn't my intention for it to be this way, but we were so desperate for you to join us here."

Jason crossed his arms. "You could have just asked."

"We couldn't be certain you'd say yes."

"Surely what you did goes against your religion."

"We do what we have to do for the safety of the galaxy," Brukan said.

"The safety of the galaxy?" Jason rubbed his temples. "What the hell are you talking about?"

Brukan gestured to the stone bench, and the trio sat beside each other. "This world, believe it or not, is one of the last bastions of the Retebu civilization."

Jason glanced around the temple. "You're saying the Retebu once lived here?"

"Some did, yes. Millions of years ago. When the final war between the Retebu and the Kalceni erupted across the galaxy, some found refuge on this planet."

"What happened to them?"

"They died like the rest of their race. This world was as inhospitable then as it is now. But they were so desperate, they had no choice but to settle down. Their physiology just didn't cope with the conditions. In the time they spent here, they built places like this."

"So, those Retebu founded the Firstborn religion?"

Brukan nodded. "When the Plauvians came across this world, the doctrines of the word of the Firstborns were found. They weren't only an instruction manual on the Retebu way of life, but a warning of those called the Kalceni."

"And the prophecies?" Jason said. "The Retebu had eyes on the future with the spheres, didn't they?"

"Yes." Brukan flipped to a page toward the back of the book on his lap. "A time will come when darkness spreads. A Guardian will lead the people to the light, and the sins of the past will be extinguished."

"I heard those words spoken on Tadrosia."

"One of many worlds our missionaries spread the word of the Firstborns to." Brukan pointed at the ancient writing on the yellowed parchment. "Scholars here on Plauvia believe this prophecy describes the Kalceni attack on the Alliance with the Retebu sphere.

And ultimately their defeat at the hands of the Guardian Kione."

A lump formed in Jason's throat at the sound of his friend's name.

Brukan turned another page. "The seeds of destruction will give rise to the inner darkness. A new fight will be waged. It will be the final battle."

Jason narrowed his eyes at the old text. "When I was on Mascoros Prime, a Firstborn cleric warned me of a future that sounds very much like this prophecy."

"There was no celebration amongst the followers of the Firstborns when the Kalceni were defeated, because we knew this darkness would inevitably arise."

"You're talking about planets seceding from the Alliance? Conflicts arising from old rivalries?"

"Yes, Jason." Brukan closed the book. "While the Kalceni might be gone, their ideas still linger. And those ideas are being employed today by the weak-minded. Since their destruction, the fabric of this galaxy has been slowly unwoven. Order is giving way to chaos, just as the Kalceni had always wanted. Chaos to the weak is power."

"Your book is filled with prophecies. What's supposed to happen next?"

"Unfortunately, the prophecies in these pages were never completed." Brukan frowned. "The words I spoke are but the final written by the Retebu before their civilization here on Retebu perished. What comes next is up to us. We must heal the galaxy before it spirals out of the control."

Jason stood and paced around the lectern. "I've seen what the Retebu are capable of in death, and the power of their spheres, so I don't disbelieve anything you're telling me. But when you bought me here, you claimed I could help you. How can that possibly be?"

Brukan glanced at Mirin. "He has no idea, does he?"

She shook her head. "No."

The cleric stood and motioned toward the temple door. "Come, Jason. It's time."

THIRTY-FOUR

Brielaro

Javier stood in the viewing gallery overlooking the Company ship's hangar deck as yet another transport pod arrived from the surface. The side airlock opened, and members of the expedition guided more hover lifters of relics from the dig. Most items he'd already seen for himself on Planet Zero, but a few were new. His colleagues had obviously been hard at work.

"Fantastic, isn't it?"

Javier flinched, startled from the voice behind him. He spun around to find Onlor traipsing toward him from the shadows as if an eagle about to feast on its prey. He joined him, checking out the latest haul.

"Never in my wildest dreams would I have ever thought we'd come to take possession of this much Kalceni technology," the expedition leader said. "I can't thank you enough for that."

Javier frowned. "What do you plan to do with it?"

"My goals are the same as yours. We're here to further our horizons by studying it."

"Hmm."

"Is there something you'd like to say to me, Professor?" Onlor stepped in front of him, blocking his view of the hangar deck. "This is about the communiqué you had with your friend Faranar, isn't it?"

Javier's heart skipped a beat. "You know about that?"

"There's nothing that happens on this ship I don't know about."

Javier wondered if Kranlar relayed the communiqué to his commanding officer, or if Onlor had been keeping tabs on him all on his own from the very beginning. "I had questions that had to be answered."

"Yes, well, I suppose I should have expected that from such a curious mind." Onlor returned to Javier's side and stared back out at the men and women under his command, continuing to unload the transport pod. "You didn't expect to find what you did, I assume?"

"I knew something was up, I just wasn't certain what. I won't ask you the nitty-gritty on how you got your hands on a Company ship, but I must know what your true intentions are out here."

Onlor crossed his arms and sighed. "You remember when I came to you on Earth?"

Javier nodded.

"You'll recall me telling you about the roadblocks I'd

faced with the Alliance Council denying me an expedition to the Kalceni base?" he continued.

"Of course. I gather they never changed their mind on that."

"They didn't. That's why I did what I did. I was desperate. I wasn't ever going to get permission, so I put in my resignation and took matters into my own hands. I had enough people willing to come with me, and the rest is history." Onlor placed his hand on the window, fixated on the relics. "The Kalceni are a mystery no one in the Alliance understands. That's incredibly dangerous. No species in the galaxy would have achieved what they have from being so timid. If you were in my position, and believed the only way we could ever fight off a future Kalceni attack was to learn more about them, what would you have done?"

Javier raised his eyebrows. "You're asking if I would have gone against the orders of my superiors?"

Onlor nodded.

"Before recruiting me on this expedition, you surely looked into my history," Javier said. "You must know I was locked up for my hand in helping Jason Cassidy escape the clutches of President Jarret."

The Ulvekan smiled. "You and I aren't so different, Professor."

Javier's skin crawled.

"I've always been an Alliance man," Onlor told him. "However, since the Kalceni attack, the Alliance I grew up with has changed. To not want to know more about its enemy is ludicrous. The bureaucrats running it have become weak. So, I figured if they weren't going to do anything about it, I would."

Javier thought about everything he'd witnessed since arriving aboard the *Brielaro*. "While I don't agree with what you've done, I can at least understand the position you're coming from."

"Professor, I wouldn't have asked you on this expedition if it wasn't for your expertise. But there was another reason I wanted you here with me."

"Oh?"

"Of all the species I've worked with and met over my lifetime, humans still have something few of them have."

"What's that?"

"The thirst for knowledge." Onlor balled his hand into a fist. "I know how uncomfortable it was for you to return to the Kalceni base, especially with everything you've gone through since Orion V. But I knew you'd do it because of the traits so ingrained in humanity. You understand how important it is that we continue our work on Planet Zero. Can you allow me to repair the trust between us? Can you let me show you the importance of what we're here for?"

Javier gazed through the window at the last of the relics being shipped from the transport pod. "What do you need me to do?"

Onlor motioned from the viewing gallery, and they made their way back to the briefing room. Unlike earlier, it was completely empty. Their footsteps echoed against the bulkheads, and Onlor walked behind his seat at the head of the table, activating the hologram above. An image appeared of the building they'd discovered on Planet Zero buried beneath the sand. All the passageways they'd explored were colored in yellow, along with the library toward the bottom of the ruin.

"A team on the surface has been working with our holographic Kalceni librarian, and she's given us a better picture of what the ruins looked like before the attack by the Retebu." Onlor zoomed out, and the warped building returned to an upright position. Other buildings surrounded it, making up the rest of the vast metropolis. "Considering the condition of the building we found, one must assume most of this city has likely been destroyed, or at the very least, buried so deep it'll make excavation difficult. Regardless, the librarian has provided us with directions to the laboratory, which was home of the Eternal Plan before the Kalceni attack. It may be there. It may not. Either way, I intend to find out."

Javier pricked up his ears at the designation of the project, which gave the Kalceni the ability to move their consciousness from one being to another. He shifted closer to the table and narrowed his eyes at the red line from the bottom of the building down what would have once been a street to the smaller structure marked as the laboratory.

"I don't know what we'll find down there, Professor," Onlor said. "But if there's something there, if there is the secret to how these beings became immortal, I need the best mind with me when I do it. Will you come with me?"

Javier peered through the translucent hologram at the man who had put everything on the line to get to where he was. While he was still incredibly wary of the Ulvekan, Onlor was right about him. "The unknown is a siren song impossible for me to ignore."

THIRTY-FIVE

Plauvia

Plauvia seemed so flat from orbit, but since Jason's arrival, and especially on his trek from the temple, he'd discovered it had much more contours than met the eye. He wouldn't have minded climbing up a few hills, but scaling the numerous sand dunes really gave him a workout he didn't expect. His calves burned, and his lower back ached from bending down to claw his way up the finely grained mounds.

Jason was relatively fit, all things being equal, so he knew he'd get over it, but he felt for the four apprentices who were carrying Brukan up and down the dunes on a very basic litter. Hover vehicles didn't appear to be the flavor of the month on Plauvia. No technology did, for that matter.

Jason caught up to Mirin who had broken away from the pack and took in a series of deep breaths. She continued on at a steady pace, without even panting. "How aren't you breaking a sweat?" he asked her.

"I grew up here," she said. "We have no choice but to adapt to our surroundings."

"Is this where you learned how to fight as well?"

"The martial arts I studied since I was a child have been handed down from generation to generation. Some say it's based on old Retebu doctrines, while others claim its Plauvian in origin. No one knows."

"So, you could be fighting in the same style the Retebu once did six million years ago?"

"Possibly. I've concluded it's a mixture of the two. A fusion of two cultures' prowess. One thing is certain, however—it's to only be used when absolutely necessary."

Jason chuckled. "Was it absolutely necessary in that bar back on Myjurna Station?"

Mirin didn't stop, taking the longest strides possible for her small size, staying one step ahead of him. "You're speaking of the alien that attacked you in the bar?"

"I figure it must have been a setup."

She said nothing at first, appearing to gather her thoughts. "Yes, I paid him to start the brawl with you."

"Unbelievable."

"I can't apologize any more for the way I've treated you. Honestly, I wish I could. But as Brukan said, this was all necessary to ensure you came to Plauvia." Mirin paused. "I specifically asked him not to do any long-term damage."

Jason winced, recalling the beating and the bruises he'd ended up with. "He hurt enough."

"I needed to gain your trust. Originally my plan was to ask for passage, or stow away on the *Argo* and abduct you in your sleep, but when I discovered you were looking for an extra crew member, I figured that was the best chance to get aboard your ship."

"The whole production wasn't a setup, was it? The Treviens. The Quarons. Our rescue of Doctor Tai. That had nothing to do with you, right?"

"Those incidents were simply bad luck. Though hardly surprising, considering the stories of your time out here. None of them were my doing. If anything, they only hindered my mission in bringing you here."

"I still wish you'd asked," Jason grumbled.

"I promise next time I get sent to abduct you from your vessel, I'll ask first."

Jason widened his eyes. It was the first joke he'd heard her crack since they'd met. "I didn't think it was possible..."

The pair continued ahead of the others through the desert, until they reached another region of rock formations, similar to where the temple had been built by the Retebu six million years earlier.

"You've got to tell me, Mirin, why did the Plauvians decide to settle on this world?" Jason asked her, stopping by a boulder and resting on it.

She finally came to a halt, too, and peered at the rest of the party, who were some way behind them. "My people were once great explorers. Plauvians are a very old race. Nowhere near as ancient as the Retebu or the Kalceni, but we inhabited the stars long before the thought of an Alliance was ever considered. We roamed the heavens, discovered new worlds, and were quite technologically advanced."

Jason couldn't help but stare at the blue apprentice robes she'd changed into. He'd since learned those who donned the particular garb would either become clerics or missionaries to spread the word of the Firstborns throughout the galaxy. "Technologically advanced? What happened?"

"The extinction."

Jason raised both eyebrows.

Mirin pulled a bottle of water from her pack and offered it to Jason. "Our original home, Old Plauvia, was destroyed by an environmental cataclysm. We used our world and its resources to the point it could not take our abuse any longer. When my ancestors discovered the planet we're standing on now, and the word of the Firstborns, they saw it as a second chance. Those that settled here on New Plauvia, or Plauvia as it became to be called over time, decided to live a simpler life, casting aside much of their technology. They used the teachings of the Firstborns to become one with their new world."

Jason chugged down some water. "Surely you could have picked a more welcoming place."

"I believe the Plauvians settled on this planet as a way of paying penance for what they'd done to their original home. Every youngling that grows up goes through the trials of living on this world and devotes themselves to existing as one with their environment."

Jason thought back to another devastated place he'd visited on his journey in search of his brother. "That's why you send missionaries out into the galaxy, to places like Tadrosia. You don't want anyone else making the same mistakes?"

"That's correct. But we also like to have our eyes and ears out there to know what's happening beyond the orbit of this world."

Jason darted his eyes sideways at the shuffling sands. Brukan and the rest of his party approached and pointed ahead of them through the rocks.

"We're close," the cleric said.

Everyone continued on, and the rocks eventually became so high that the horizon disappeared behind them. They walked downward until they reached what appeared almost like an amphitheater lost to time. At the bottom of the stone steps was a flat, circular area with some clustered rocks protruding from the ground. Like those around it, there was a form and functionality to it.

Brukan's apprentices let him down from his litter, and the old cleric went toward the clustered rocks. He invited Jason and Mirin forward, and they joined him. Jason froze as soon as he saw the markings scrawled on them.

"I've seen these pictographs before," he said. "On the Retebu sphere."

Brukan nodded. "This is but another Retebu device left behind."

"What does it do?"

"The scholars believe it's a communicator."

Jason glanced at the commband on his wrist. "That's one mighty communicator."

Brukan smiled wryly. "It's believed to work on a slightly different principle to the mechanism around your wrist."

"So, what's it used for?"

"If the inscriptions displayed on it are correct, it's here if we should ever need to talk with a Guardian."

Jason looked into the collection of rocks. Inside was the perfect area for someone to lie down in it. "Does it work?"

"We don't know. In all the years we've tried, it hasn't functioned for us. It's said that only a Retebu or someone touched by the Retebu can use the communicator."

Jason delved deep into his mind at everything that had happened since Mirin had brought him to Plauvia. "That's why you need my help?"

"You were touched by the Retebu, Jason." Brukan placed his hands together. "You've linked minds with the one known as Kione. If there's anyone that can use the communicator, it will be you."

Jason turned back to the ancient device and rubbed the outer stone. It was just as rough and coarse as the rest of the rocks he'd come across on Plauvia. "This is some serious mumbo-jumbo."

Mirin stepped to his side. "We discussed the eyes and the ears we've planted beyond this world. We understand how deeply wounded the galaxy is, and the damage taking place because of the Kalceni. Our clerics on Plauvia have concluded that we have no choice but to reach out to the Guardians for help."

Jason stared at the device and thought of the last time he'd seen his friend on Earth, before he'd shimmered away to wherever, somewhere far away from him. "So, you're saying I could see Kione by lying on this communicator?"

"That's our hope," Brukan said.

"Will you help us, Jason?" Mirin asked him.

He sighed at all the expectant faces. "How do I get in this thing?"

THIRTY-SIX

Cargo Ship Argo

Aly stared at the white chess piece in her hand as the trans-space corridor shone through the viewport, bathing her in its beautiful colors. It felt as if she'd been standing there for hours. In reality, it had only been a few minutes. She'd visited every part of the ship since being harassed by the Jahjina, making it necessary for the *Argo* to go the long way around to reach Plauvia.

No matter how much she roamed the vessel, trying to keep her mind clear, she couldn't stop thinking about Jason and why Mirin had taken him. She played back everything in her head since they'd first met the woman in the bar on Myjurna Station. Aly always assumed she was a pretty good judge of character and immediately thought Mirin a worthy addition to their crew. She'd never held that opinion of anyone else who had joined the cargo ship in all the years she'd grown up aboard her. Somehow those intuitions had failed her. She threw the chess piece at the board, and it clattered into the others, knocking them to the floor.

Her commband flashed, alerting her to how close the *Argo* was to their destination. She left the rec room and returned to the bridge to find her dad sitting at the helm and Althaus at the systems station. Doctor Tai stood near the captain's chair, propping herself up with her crutches. Aly wondered how much longer the woman would need the aid. In a very short space of time, even with the injuries she'd sustained on Gunos, she was moving much freer than she thought possible.

They all turned to Aly as her footsteps echoed around the bridge. She stopped on the opposite side of the captain's chair, and her father gave her a knowing look. Aly glanced at the vacant seat between her and the doctor. She now understood what Jason felt when Tyler had left the *Argo* to him in his will. She knew she was no imposter and capable of the job, but there was still a huge reluctance to sit in while Jason was gone.

"We're approaching the end of the trans-space corridor," her father informed her.

The *Argo* slowed from the ultra FTL speed of trans-space, and the reds and purples around them disappeared into the blackness of space. The other five gateways of the hub greeted them, along with something no one expected.

"Holy hell," Althaus muttered.

"That's a lot of ships," her dad said, cautiously steering them clear of those near to them.

"How many are there?" Tai asked.

Aly glanced at the systems station. "Althaus?"

He checked his scanners. "I'm detecting at least three hundred Alliance bogeys, with dozens of varied designs and configurations."

"What could they be doing here?" Tai pondered.

"They could be here for several different reasons," Aly's father said. "With all the issues happening throughout the Alliance at the moment, they could be on some kind of mission."

"Althaus, are any of those ships pointing their guns at us?" Aly asked.

He shook his head. "They probably don't even realize we're here amongst all of this."

"Good. What about the route to Plauvia? Is the gateway being blocked?"

"We've got a clear path."

"That's what I wanted to hear. Dad, plot a course."

He nodded from the helm and ran his hands over the controls. The *Argo* moved off and weaved through the various ships converging with one another and forming smaller groups.

Aly narrowed her eyes on the fleet and thought back to the chess set in the rec room. Someone, somewhere was playing with massive pieces and placing them into position. For what purpose, she didn't know. Right now, she didn't care.

"Approaching the gateway," her dad said.

The vortex came to life in front of them, and the *Argo* entered.

Planet Zero

Javier lost count of how many times he'd traveled between the *Brielaro* and the surface of Planet Zero. One thing was for certain, however. He was getting sick of the heat.

The transport touched down, and he and Onlor exited through the airlock with a pair of guards brought down from the ship. On the sands around them in the midday sun, the rest of the expedition party continued collecting the relics from the ruins.

The team of four led by Onlor walked to the entrance near the spire and climbed through the small hatch. The sun disappeared and was replaced with the artificial lighting set up on the walls of the ancient structure. They moved past the office-like spaces on the observation level and burrowed farther underground to the bottom of the building.

Along the way they came across other members of the expedition, but also excavation personnel hard at work. Eventually the foursome reached the library, and the guards took a position on each side of the door. Onlor went to the center of the room and pushed down on the circular plate he had when they'd first discovered the well-maintained section of the ruin.

The same bright light emanated from the ceiling, and the translucent figure of the Kalceni hologram took shape in front of him.

"You have returned," she greeted them with a cheerful smile.

Javier struggled to wrap his head around the computerized life form. With everything he'd seen of the Kalceni, he couldn't ever imagine a member of their race being so pleasant.

"What can I assist you with today?" the librarian asked.

"I have a team of excavators who are slowly making their way toward the laboratory you claim is the home of the Eternal Plan," Onlor said.

She raised her hand and brought up the holographic map shown to Javier in the briefing room aboard the *Brielaro*. It twisted and melded to appear more like the ruins they were currently standing in, with many of the buildings either missing or squashed from the forces above. "My sensors detect your machinery is having trouble finding the entrance to the laboratory."

Onlor nodded. "It seems the laboratory is not where you claimed it to be."

His terseness didn't seem to faze her programming, and she zoomed in on the region where the machines had stopped. "I did warn you due to the passage of time, the laboratory might have been lost."

"I understand that, but if it hasn't—"

"Do you require assistance?" she asked. "I can come with you, if you'd like."

Onlor and Javier raised their eyebrows.

She waved her hand again, and the map disappeared. Another opening appeared in the floor, and a pill-shaped device the size of a hand shot from it and hovered near Onlor's fingertips. He reached out and yanked it from thin air. Javier stepped closer to him, and the pair inspected the object, which had no buttons or screen of any type on it.

"As long as you carry that with you, I'll be able to accompany you," she said.

Onlor smiled and handed it to Javier, who placed it in his pocket. "Then, let's go."

THIRTY-SEVEN

Plauvia

Mirin helped Jason onto the communicator and placed his hands on two round rocks at his fingertips.

"This is even more uncomfortable than it looked in the brochure," he said, attempting to find a position upright where his ass didn't feel numb from the flat slab.

Mirin and Brukan exchanged odd glances with their wrinkled eyebrows, which Jason could only assume was the Plauvian way of rolling their eyes.

"Try to lie down," the cleric instructed him.

Jason lay backward and peered up into the cloudy Plauvian sky. While the sun was farther off to the west, the glare was intense, forcing him to close his eyes ever so slightly. "Is something supposed to have happened yet?"

"You need to relax," Mirin told him.

"I am relaxed."

"You're all tensed up."

"Well, maybe you should teach me some of that meditation stuff you were doing on the *Argo*."

"It would take you decades to learn, let alone master."

"I've been told I'm a quick learner."

Brukan reached over and put a hand on his shoulder. "Close your eyes, Jason."

He stared deep into the cleric's eyes and for a moment swore he got lost inside them. Eventually Jason's eyelids closed, and the muscles in his body relaxed. The warm slab of the communicator even began to feel like his bed back on the *Argo*.

Aly!

His eyes shot open to find Mirin and Brukan still standing on either side of him. The eldest of the pair patted his shoulder again, and Jason tried to calm himself. The sky disappeared, and the sliver of brightness remaining turned to black as his eyelids closed over.

"Now breathe deeply," Brukan said. "In and out."

Jason gulped in the thin air of the desert planet and remained as still as he possibly could. His head became faint, and everything began to spin. Then in the darkness, a spark of light blinked beyond him, and Brukan's soft touch disappeared.

Another flash struck.

He opened his eyes.

But there was only the night.

He was still on the ancient Retebu communicator, but the sun had shifted, and bursts of lightning flared in the distance against the desert's sandy dunes.

Brukan and Mirin were gone, too.

"Hello?" Jason called out.

A clap of thunder cracked.

More lightning flashed.

"Mirin!" he yelled. "Brukan?"

No one answered, and the storm quickly closed in on him.

He tried to get up from the slab, but a transparent bubble grew around him and restrained him on the communicator. He pushed against it, but it threw him down on his back.

Above, the brightest strike of lightning struck only meters away from him, along with an almighty boom of thunder.

Then the ground quaked.

And it didn't stop.

The reverberation jangled through the slab and up into his body, swaying him like a tree in a tempest. His surroundings spun around him, and he closed his eyes, doing all he could to avoid vomiting. He put his hands on his ears as the violent winds nearly deafened him.

Then everything stopped.

The shaking.

The howling.

The spinning.

Jason slowly opened his eyes, and above, the daylight sky appeared. But it was different. It wasn't as bright. He assumed it was later in the day and the sun had moved farther west.

But something wasn't right.

There were less clouds. They were whiter, and fluffier.

Beneath him, the communicator had disappeared and was replaced with lush green grass. And instead of the surrounding amphitheater, there were trees. Tall ones. Just as vividly colored as the grass.

He slowly heaved himself upright and rubbed his back. "Where the hell am I?"

Attempting to move, he marched onward. In an instant, everything blurred around him before quickly coming back into focus.

"What the...?"

Jason spun to find a spherical bubble over the patch of grass he'd awoken on. He trudged toward it and put a fingertip on the translucence, pushing through it as if it were water.

He peered up into the sky at the two dots of light near the horizon, representing binary stars. Jason recalled the communicator on Plauvia, a world with only one sun, and questioned if Brukan had got it all wrong.

What if it's not a communicator at all?

He wondered if it was actually a transport device, because he certainly wasn't on Plauvia anymore. Without understanding any of the physics around it, he yanked his hand back from the bubble and turned toward the forest.

In the distance, through the gentle breeze flinging the leaves from the trees, a rushing sound danced across the air. He followed it through the undergrowth of the forest, passing by the towering trees with ungodly thick trunks, and plowing through the squelching muck until he reached a clearing.

Beyond it lay a river with a harsh current forcing the water downstream. Jason stopped at the edge and gazed at the other side. Without trusting his swimming abilities to get him over, he walked along the river until he came across a huge uprooted tree, acting as a bridge. He climbed up the gigantic log, nearly slipping from the moss which had grown on top of it. He pressed onward ever so carefully, treating it like a tightrope.

Jason eventually reached the far side and jumped down on to the equally muddy ground beneath. Without looking backward, he continued to another forested area with the same rotted leaves filling the undergrowth, dropping him almost ankle deep in some parts.

Then he stumbled on a rock.

He craned his neck around and hauled himself out of the muck. But the rock was shiny. He returned to his hands and knees to dig it out. With several scoops, he lifted the object and scraped the dirt away.

That's no rock...

It was smooth on its face and jagged at its edges.

As he headed farther onward, he found more of the metallic debris. Some as small as his hand. Others as large as his torso. He put the first piece of alloy under his arm and moved out into another open expanse, filled with long grass, stopping at the top of a ridge.

Ahead in the distance, something just as man-made

as the pieces of metal he'd found pushed through the abundant greenness of the alien world.

A ship?

Jason couldn't determine its shape from its woeful condition, but it was definitely a space vehicle of some kind. With the growth around it, it had likely been there for months. Probably years.

THIRTY-EIGHT

In all his exuberance, Jason almost slipped on the wet grass beneath his feet. Even out in the open, the dampness of an earlier downpour drenched his path.

He moved down the ridge as safely as he could, keeping his hands low to stop himself from falling over, and made his way toward the downed ship. But he stopped halfway when some brightness caught the corner of his eye. One or both of the suns in the sky reflected against something in the distance. He figured it couldn't hurt to investigate. The vessel certainly wasn't going anywhere in a hurry.

When he reached the site, the reflection disappeared from the changing angle, but there was no doubt what he'd stumbled upon. There in front of him, protruding from the ground, were over a dozen wooden posts made of the same timber as the trees from the forest. And around one of them hung a diamond necklace.

He wandered over to it and held the small piece of jewelry in his hand. Beneath it on the post were the letters: JTH. The other posts had similar initials on them, too. He'd unfortunately visited too many graveyards in his time to get it confused with anything else.

He might not have known any of the fallen, but it proved one thing. Since the initials were all in English, the crashed ship was undoubtedly from the commonwealth.

Jason put the necklace back in its rightful spot and returned toward the vessel, to an inviting hatchway on what appeared to be its starboard side. It was all bent out of shape, likely from the impact, but it was open. He hunched through it and dropped slightly, finding the craft sunken into the ground.

There was a rancid smell in the dark confines of the unknown ship. The deck was littered with dead leaves, grass, and the bulkheads were stripped almost bare of their housings. Wanting some light, Jason peeked his head into a nearby maintenance hatch and played around with the basic circuitry. It was all commonwealth components.

"Wish you were here, Aly," he muttered, stopping what he was doing and thinking about her and the others.

They're probably worried sick.

He could only imagine what they must be thinking.

They wouldn't even know where I am.

Or if I'm alive.

He sighed and rerouted some power to see if any juice was still available. Suddenly a faint beam of light emanated from the ceiling and bathed the rest of the corridor in a dim glow. "Well, I'll be damned. There must be some battery power still left in this old thing after all."

He set off and stopped by the first door, pushing it inward. Due to the age and the wear from the weather, it creaked, but he swung it all the way just the same.

Inside he found little more than darkness, relying on the lighting fixtures from the corridor to reveal the room's function. He entered using his hands to feel his way around until his eyes got used to his surroundings. When they finally did, he discovered a row of beds, a counter, and several cabinets confirming he'd entered the ship's infirmary. Finding nothing to explain why the ship was there, he moved back into the corridor to a junction where a ladder ran from the deck above to another level below.

More light gleamed through at the top of the chute, so he took it as a sign and climbed the rungs upward to the next deck, where more of the emergency fixtures emanated with a dull glow. It was similar in shape to the other deck. But there were more doors. He entered one to find a typical set of quarters. It felt lived-in despite the damage. He thought back to the graveyard he'd stumbled upon and gathered the cabin belonged to one of the unfortunate souls who had been buried.

The next door opened into the ship's mess hall. It wasn't as compact as the *Argo's* galley, or anywhere near as big as a mess hall on any of the CDF ships he'd served, but there was no doubt about its function with the servery on the far wall and tables throughout. The remnants of rotted food stained the deck along with up-ended chairs scattered across the deck.

"Hello!" Jason called out.

Only his echo replied.

He shook his head and left, climbing another deck via the ladder chute. At both ends of the ship's top level were hatchways, while tiny viewports lining the corridor looked out onto the wilderness of the planet.

Jason went through the forward hatchway to the bridge. The lights were out, but the suns beamed through the viewport, giving him a full picture of the command center. He passed the captain's chair and stopped at the helm, brushing aside the dust and grime which had collected on the controls. He prodded at the buttons. But they were just as dead as everything else he'd come across since making his way aboard.

Jason turned and peered around the rest of the bridge at all the chairs which were swiveled toward the various stations.

All were empty.

Except one.

He cautiously stepped to the seat with a pair of feet planted on the deck beneath it and gently spun it around, revealing a decomposed body in shabby clothes sitting before him.

Jason flinched at the ghastly sight before edging closer to the skeleton. "I suppose someone had to dig all those graves, didn't they?"

He examined the console behind the body and

reached for a little black book lying on the keypad. He brushed the dust from it and opened the first page.

"*Bombay*?" he read from it, tilting his head sideways. He flicked the page to find more text, this time in almost perfect block handwriting. "The Diary of Doctor Benjamin Tyrell."

Jason dropped the little black book to his side and remembered the somber day when the *Raptor* engaged the *Bombay* with the strict instructions to destroy it and the Centauri war criminals aboard her. It wasn't until later he'd discovered the truth that they were in fact just escaping President Jarret who'd wanted him to create super soldiers with Kione's alien DNA. He turned another page to find the first entry. When he moved to get some more light from the viewport, his jaw dropped open.

A figure stood before him, casting a shadow across his body.

Jason let go of the diary, and it plummeted to his feet.

"Kione?"

THIRTY-NINE

"I suppose I should have known I'd find you here."

Jason stared at his friend, who appeared as an apparition just like the last time he'd seen him at his home in the Sierra Nevada Mountains. However, there was something different about him. While Kione didn't display his emotions as loosely as humans, there was a darkness in his features which Jason had never encountered before.

"What are you doing here?" Kione asked him without so much as a smile.

"Is that all you've got to say to me?" he said, startled by the directness of the Retebu. "Not, how are you? What have you been up to? Watched any good movies lately?"

Kione glared at him. Another expression rarely seen on his friend's face.

Jason gestured around the bridge. "Where are we?"

"You're aboard the *Bombay*."

"I know that. I also know that's Doctor Tyrell sitting

over there." Jason stopped at the solemness in the alien's eyes. "I'm sorry. I didn't mean to be so blunt."

Kione frowned and walked to the front of the bridge next to the *Bombay's* viewport.

"What happened here?" Jason asked.

Kione put his hands behind his back and stared out at the beautiful green vista. "You remember the day that the *UECS Raptor* tracked the *Bombay* down at Nebula TPA-338?"

"You know I do. That's where all this wackiness began."

"And you'll also recall Christian Nash was pulled into the trans-space corridor of the Kalceni ship?"

"Of course." Jason joined Kione's side at the viewport. "Is that what happened here?"

"Not exactly." Kione sighed. "From what I've been able to piece together with Doctor Tyrell's diary and some other records throughout the *Bombay*, it would appear, yes, they were pulled into a vortex, but it was the exit vortex of the Kalceni ship, not the entry vortex which took Christian Nash's pod to Psi-Aion."

"So, the Kalceni had traveled from somewhere else prior to Nebula TPA-338?"

"We know they were searching for the Retebu sphere for a long time. They probably went to all four corners of the galaxy."

"Makes sense." Jason rubbed his chin. "And what planet is this exactly?"

"It has no official designation in Earth records. Or

even Alliance ones for that matter, as its far beyond their borders."

"In other words, we're a long way away from anywhere?"

"Indeed."

"So, they were sucked through the trans-space vortex and crash-landed here? Then what? Was Tyrell the only one who made it?"

Kione shook his head. "Remarkably, it appears most of the crew survived. It was Mother Nature on this planet that was their ultimate demise. As the first few perished, Doctor Tyrell believed there was something in the water. They designed a filtration system, but more died. He eventually surmised it was a toxin in the planet's air. Without the resources to determine his theory, he couldn't develop an antidote. One by one they fell until they were all buried beneath the ground."

Jason glanced over his shoulder at Doctor Tyrell's ghastly body in the chair. "I suppose this is not what you expected to find when you went looking for him."

Kione joined him, peering across at the man. "When I first came here, I immediately thought of you."

Jason raised his eyebrows.

"When you hunted for clues to what happened to Christian Nash, you never truly knew what you were going to discover either. But you did it out of a loyalty to a friend, because he would have done the same for you. While I didn't wish to find this, at least he got to live his last days in a quaint paradise away from the grasp of President Jarret."

Jason reached out to put a comforting hand on Kione's shoulder, but not thinking about it, forgot the advanced life form was without physical shape, and his hand simply passed through him.

Cargo Ship Argo

Kevin remained at the helm controls as the tip-tapping footsteps of his daughter paced constantly behind him. The pair had said barely anything to each other since Mirin had abducted Jason. There had been so little time with all the hoops they'd been forced to jump through. Though he wondered how much he could really say.

He was just as worried as her, and just as fearful at what might have happened to the man that was once a young boy who could barely fit in the very seat Kevin was now sitting in. He was like a son to him. His best friend Benjamin asked him to look after both Tyler and Jason when he passed. And while Tyler was still alive, there was a pang of guilt at what had happened to him on Rixiia that would haunt Kevin to the day he died. With Jason being snatched from under their noses, he couldn't help but feel he'd failed twice.

The helm beeped, and he stopped feeling sorry for himself. He checked his monitor and turned to Alyssa, who stood next to the captain's chair. "This trans-space corridor is coming to an end," Kevin informed her. "One more changeover and we'll be on our way to Plauvia."

The *Argo* emerged from the gateway into normal space. Kevin had to pull up quickly, blasting the ship's forward thrusters as another large group of vessels appeared in their path.

"Now, who the hell are these guys?" Althaus muttered.

Alyssa walked over to Althaus and checked his scanners. "That's the Swanilli," she said.

Kevin nodded, recognizing the design on his monitor of people they'd done business with before. "I remember them being quite a kind and generous race who didn't venture that far from their home."

"They're pacifists, aren't they?" Tai asked from the operations station.

"If they were, they're not anymore," Althaus said. "From these readings, their ships are fully loaded with some of the best firepower I've seen on any Alliance ship."

"And they're going to Plauvia," Kevin informed everyone, examining their flight path through the next gateway.

Althaus's console beeped, and he looked up at Alyssa. "There's a ship breaking off and heading in our direction. They're opening a commlink."

"Not again." Alyssa rolled her eyes. "Put them on."

"Unknown vessel, you have strayed into territory now claimed by the Swanilli Confederacy," the voice relayed through the bridge speakers. *"You are ordered to leave immediately."*

"This is Aly Rycroft of the *Cargo Ship Argo*. I will not—"

"They've cut the commlink," Althaus told her.

"Already?"

"They're closing fast with their crosshairs locked on to us."

"I wouldn't have thought pacifism was something you could flip on and off like a light switch," Kevin quipped.

"We have to turn around," Althaus said.

Alyssa clenched her fists. "We can't keep doing this."

Kevin tapped his fingers on his console. "Perhaps we don't have to."

Alyssa approached him, putting one hand on the back of his chair and the other on the helm console. "What are you suggesting?"

"Do you trust me?" he said to her.

"Of course."

"Good." Kevin punched in a series of commands, and the *Argo* turned on a dime toward the gateway in which they'd come. He pushed the cargo ship at the heart of the hollow ring which had deactivated its trans-space vortex.

"What are we doing exactly?" his daughter asked.

"No time for chitchat." He glanced sideways at Althaus, who seemed to be just as oblivious as the others on the bridge. "When I give the order, I want you to switch all the ship's systems off. All I want is the maneuvering thrusters and helm controls."

Althaus ruffled his brow, placing his hands on the systems station and readying for the command.

Kevin checked the scanners to find the Swanilli behind them but still facing their direction. Ahead, the ring remained devoid of the trans-space activity, but he knew it would come.

As they maneuvered ever closer, on cue, the swirling ripple of the vortex came to life, inviting them inside. Alyssa didn't move her grip from the console. Either she had an inkling of what he was doing, or she trusted him enough to not disturb him. Regardless, Kevin kept the *Argo* pointed at the center of the anomaly, until he reached as far as he could without being pulled in.

"Althaus, now!" he yelled.

His old comrade did as instructed, and every light and console on the bridge blinked out, along with the hum of the sub-light engines. The *Argo's* hull groaned and squealed, and Kevin stabbed at the maneuvering thrusters, propelling the ship downward, lurching them sharply away from the vortex.

"You sly devil," Alyssa murmured. "Do you think it'll work?"

Kevin didn't answer her immediately, instead concentrating on the controls. He altered their heading again once they cleared the bottom edge of the gateway and punched the *Argo* in an upward trajectory. "Only if I can get this done before that vortex closes."

He edged the vessel closer to the far side of the gateway and maneuvered the *Argo* toward the rear of the ring. With a deft hand, he forced the ship toward it and latched on to the tough exterior of the gateway. The thud reverberated around the *Argo*, and everyone on the bridge held on to whatever was closest to them with bated breaths.

Then the vortex extinguished.

No one moved.

No one uttered a sound.

The scanners beeped, and Kevin smiled. He peered up at his daughter, who spotted it as well. "They're returning to their fleet."

Doctor Tai scratched her head. "Am I to assume that you somehow made us invisible to the Swanilli?"

"Kind of," Kevin said. "We know the scanners aboard Alliance ships are much more advanced than our own, but if there's one thing I've seen when we've dealt with them, it's that they have trouble with the gateway's energy particles. By turning off all our systems, we'd normally still be detected, but against the backdrop of the vortex, we would have appeared to have entered the gateway's trans-space corridor."

"Genius." Alyssa grasped her father's shoulder and returned to the side of the captain's chair. "Once all the Swanilli ships have moved through the vortex, switch the old girl back on and follow them in."

FORTY

Undesignated Planet

"You haven't told me why you're here."

Jason crossed his arms and leaned up against the console on the starboard side of the *Bombay's* bridge opposite Kione. "I think you know why I'm here."

The Retebu man raised his eyebrows. "You need my help?"

"Me? No. If it were that simple, I would've just found an AA meeting somewhere. It's a bit more complicated than that. This is about everyone."

Kione closed his eyes.

"Do you have any idea what's going on out there?" Jason asked. "Everything is coming apart at the seams."

"I know what's happening." Kione reopened his eyes. "Ever since the Kalceni reappeared, the balance of the galactic order has altered. They've become much more powerful in death than they could have been, even with the power of the spheres. They've obtained an immortality beyond immortality."

"We were told that their primary objective was to create chaos throughout the galaxy. It would seem that's been achieved." Jason tilted his head sideways as Kione sat at the helm. He wondered how he could sit when he was half invisible. But then the Retebu was standing on the deck, too. He put the question aside and stepped closer to him. "Something has to be done. I've come from—"

"Yes, I know." Kione's voice became almost monotone. "The clerics from Plauvia sent you."

"They believe you're our only hope."

"I'm sure they do. Their lives have been built around the Retebu way of life. A way of life that went extinct six million years ago. They've held on to their faith and believe their problems can be fixed by some divine being."

"Yes, I wonder how they could have figured that," Jason said sarcastically, waving his hand through his friend. "While I don't prescribe to be an expert on the Plauvians, or anything for that matter, I'm not sure you've got them as nailed down as you think. They're an intelligent people. But a people who have run out of ideas. In their book, you are a Guardian. And they need your help. That's the reason the Retebu from the past sent you into the future."

"This changes nothing, Jason." Kione shook his head. "Yes, the worlds of the Alliance have fractured, but they have chosen to do that themselves. While a lot can be said of 'darker forces' being behind it, the Kalceni are gone. My time as a Guardian has come to an end. There's no more I can do."

"But this is the chaos spoken of." Jason sat in the captain's chair and stared off with is friend. "We can't do this alone?"

Kione returned his equally terse gaze. "What would you have me do?"

"You're another form of life, unlike anything we know or understand. Aren't you all-powerful now?"

"I've evolved beyond what the Retebu once were, but that doesn't make me some kind of god who can simply wave his fairy dust over everything and change the entire galactic order."

Jason paced in front of him. "So, what? I'm supposed to return to Plauvia and tell them their Guardian has declined to help them?"

"Jason, I—"

"No, no," Jason said, cutting him off. "That's okay, Kione, you mope around here on whatever planet this is, on the edge of the god knows where, while everyone else tries to stop the intergalactic storm about to descend on us all."

Kione placed his head in his hands.

"You were pretty good at history when you were a kid, weren't you?" Jason asked him. "Remember when the Roman Empire fell? They were the shining beacon of civilization. Their culture had spread from one corner of the known world to the other. But then it all came crumbling down. What happened next?"

Kione straightened in his chair and pulled his hands off his face. "The Dark Ages."

"Right. Could you imagine what would happen if the Alliance fell? Could you even fathom what the Dark Ages on an intergalactic scale would look like?"

Kione stood and made his way to the door.

"You don't get to just walk away from this," Jason blasted him. "This isn't one of those philosophical discussions we used to have on the *Argo*. This is bigger. Much bigger than anything we could have ever comprehended."

Kione disappeared into thin air as if he hadn't even been there.

Jason sighed and picked up Tyrell's diary. "This was no way for you to meet your end. This is no way for any of it to end."

FORTY-ONE

Planet Zero

Javier almost wished he was back on the surface in the roasting sun. With all the excavation work taking place in the catacombs of the discovered ruins, he, Onlor, and the Company guards were beginning to bake inside the planet's subterranean layer.

Attempting to find the Kalceni laboratory had become a wild goose chase. While liaising with the holographic librarian, the excavators tapped several locations but continued to come up short. Javier, however, had to hand it to Onlor. He was laser-focused. The look in the Ulvekan's eyes was one he knew well, because it had stared back at him in the mirror many times throughout his career.

As their trek moved deeper into the ancient metropolis, he couldn't help but to continue to second-guess himself about the leader of the expedition who had seized the Company vessel. He still didn't trust him. Not by a longshot. And while Onlor had a very good point in a need for understanding the Kalceni, there was an unhealthiness about his infatuation. Regardless, Javier didn't have many options. Going against Onlor could have very dire consequences for him. He'd been locked up long enough in his life.

"Over here!" an excavation worker yelled out.

Onlor led Javier and the librarian to a hole that one of the mobile excavators had drilled. "It's hollow."

The librarian kneeled and held her hand over the top of it. "The laboratory is in here."

Javier pulled his scanner from his belt and checked the readings. "There's definitely some kind of construction beneath us."

Onlor appeared satisfied and snatched a rope from one of the workers. He threw it over the edge and climbed down, darting his flashlight around the new surroundings. "Get down here, Professor!"

Javier sighed and grabbed the rope, gently abseiling until his feet touched the floor below.

Onlor studied the dark confines and approached his side. "Where's the hologram?"

Before Javier could say a word, the librarian shimmered into existence beside them, not needing to use the rope like mere mortals.

"Are you sure this is the place?" Onlor asked her.

She nodded. "We're here."

"What's left of it, anyway." Javier beamed his flashlight around the room, which was in much worse condition than the original building they'd discovered farther up. It was all a bit of a mess with chairs, tables, and equipment sprawled over the floor, frozen in time. "Hardly surprising considering the depth of the facility."

Onlor put his hands on his hips. "This can't be what remains of the Eternal Project."

The librarian looked one way and then the other. She pointed to her left, and the trio set off. At the end of the room, they hunched through an awkwardly warped door and down a series of stairs where all the steps were either too big or too small because of the crush around them. At the bottom, Onlor crawled through the cramped opening, while Javier got on his hands and knees, sliding through it as best he could.

The hologram, unencumbered, passed through the wall, and joined them in a larger room. Both men waved their flashlights around it, finding the ceiling caved in on one side and workbenches broken off the walls on the other. The heart of the room was relatively intact, and sitting in the middle of it were two chambers not completely dissimilar to the ones they'd found the host bodies in on the Kalceni base back at Kappa-Magellan.

Onlor walked up to them and examined the relics, running his hand over them. "What do you make of it, Professor?"

Javier took out his scanner and directed it at the six million year-old relics. "It's difficult to tell, but the components are very similar to those on the base."

"Similar? Not the same?"

"You have to remember how long has passed between the destruction of this world and the construction of the base in orbit of that planet. As with anything, advancements were likely made with the passing of time."

Onlor glanced at the librarian, who remained standing behind them, with the same incessant smile on her face that she'd had when she was first activated. "Are these chambers what you were describing? Are we looking at the remnants of the Eternal Plan?"

"Yes." She stepped forward between the two men. "With these chambers the Kalceni intended to give themselves immortal life."

Onlor smiled. "Excellent."

Undesignated Planet

As the suns continued to move across the sky, Jason discovered he'd misread the planet's orbit. Instead of binary stars falling beyond the horizon, they were in fact rising and were now beating down on top of him. Beads of sweat ran down his forehead while he dug the last grave on the strange distant planet.

He stopped for a moment and glanced at the remains of Doctor Benjamin Tyrell lying on the hover lifter. He'd delicately placed his body on it and transported him from the wrecked *Bombay* out to the graveyard. It didn't seem fair everyone else got a burial and he didn't.

He drove the shovel into the ground and continued to plow through the dirt beneath him. Luckily, it was soft, so it wouldn't take long to create a hole big enough for the fallen doctor.

"Jason."

He jumped and turned to find Kione next to the hover lifter.

"Jesus, Kione, can you stop doing that?" Jason planted the shovel beside him. "You scared the living bejesus out of me."

"I'm sorry," the solemn alien apologized, fixing his eyes on his former mentor.

Jason sighed. "No, I'm sorry."

Kione raised his eyebrows.

"The way I treated you earlier." He gestured toward the *Bombay*. "It was unfair of me to rock up out of nowhere and guilt trip you into coming with me. You already did the impossible and were prepared to sacrifice yourself—"

"Please, Jason. This isn't necessary. In my life I've gotten quite used to the emotional outbursts of humans."

"I suppose you have." Jason chuckled and pulled out Tyrell's diary from his back pocket. "I assume you've read this?"

Kione nodded.

"An amazing story of survival...until it wasn't." He frowned and joined his friend next to Tyrell's remains. "He did a lot for the crew. If it weren't for him, they wouldn't have lasted nearly as long as they did."

"Unfortunately, in the end it wasn't quite enough."

Jason opened to the pages at the back of the diary.

"When he was the last one left, he gave up on devising a treatment and wrote about his achievements. Do you know what he claimed was his most remarkable?"

Kione darted his eyes away, no doubt knowing the answer.

"It was raising you at the Institute," Jason said. "Since he had no children of his own, he came to think of you as a son. Everything else paled in comparison to watching you grow from that small child discovered in the Galilei System, to the adult you were when he left TIAS. He praised your gentleness, your loyalty, and your forthrightness."

Kione looked back at him.

"He was right." Jason closed the diary and placed it in his pocket. "I found you to have all those qualities and more."

Kione said nothing, instead returning his gaze to the man who'd raised him.

Jason gripped the shovel firmly in his hand. "Can you give me some help? I'd like someone to speak a few words on his behalf."

FORTY-TWO

Cargo Ship Argo

Aly stood by her father's side at the helm, waiting for the trans-space corridor to dissipate. The anticipation had tied her stomach in knots, and looking down at the time on her commband only made matters worse.

"Are you okay?" her dad whispered.

Aly nodded, keeping her eyes firmly peeled on the viewport. She didn't really know what to say. She wasn't okay. And her father knew it. But talking about it on the bridge was the last thing anyone needed. She had to be focused because what happened next when they came out of the gateway would determine Jason's fate.

If he's still alive.

"Here we go," her dad said, letting everyone on the bridge know they were reaching their destination. The *Argo* drifted through the gateway and out into normal space toward the big yellow orb that was Plauvia. Aly instantly narrowed her eyes at what else was waiting for them. Not only were the ships they'd followed in a high orbit, but several more, too. So many, in fact, they dimmed out the sun.

She walked over to Althaus at the systems station and checked his readings. "Am I seeing what I think I am?"

"If you're talking about the Jahjina ships, then yes, they're identical to the ones that were blocking our path at the other gateway," he said. "I'm also picking up at least another five hundred other vessels surrounding Plauvia."

"So that's what they meant when the gateway was being used for fleet maneuvers. They were coming here all along." Aly bit down on her bottom lip. "Why in the hell are they so interested in Plauvia?"

"It can't be for anything good. These ships aren't exactly merchant carriers. They're all armed for combat."

"If Jason's down on that planet..." Aly drifted off and returned to the helm. "I don't suppose you've got any more ideas how we can get through all that?"

Her father shook his head. "I'm afraid my trick bag is only so big."

"Althaus, can you scan the planet's surface?" she asked.

"With all this activity?" He swiveled around in his chair. "Not a chance."

Aly sighed. "Are you reading any communications between the fleet and the Plauvians?"

"Nothing. Not one frequency is open. There also

doesn't appear to be any Plauvian vessels making their way from the surface to engage the enemy fleet."

Aly glanced across at Tai, who stared through the viewport just as hopeless as everyone else. "What are you thinking, Doctor?"

The older woman frowned. "Little is known about the Plauvians. They choose not to be part of the Alliance for reasons we're obviously not privy to. As to why they don't engage them; how could they possibly challenge an armada of such force?"

Planet Zero

"How does it work?"

Onlor rounded the two chambers while Javier continued to study the data on his handheld scanner. Since their holographic guide instructed them how to route the solar power from her library to the laboratory, the chambers lit up with a soft green light.

The librarian stood between them and turned to Onlor. "The Eternal Plan's directive was to move the life force of one being into another—"

"Yes, yes," he grumbled. "Everyone here understands what the Kalceni were attempting. I want to know how they did it."

The librarian pointed to the chamber on the left. "Open it."

Onlor stepped toward it and pulled the door ajar. More green illumination emanated from inside it, and Javier's scanner filled with new data. He joined the Ulvekan's side and gazed at the emerald-colored crystal fixed into the top of the chamber.

"Six million years ago, a jewel known as harstones were discovered in the ground of this world. Kalceni scientists recognized their many powers and took advantage of them. One was the ability to biologically code an individual and direct the energy into another."

Javier glanced at the information on the small screen of his scanner and then at the librarian. "Are you telling us these devices work on the basis of turning someone's life force into a data stream?"

"That's right," she said. "One individual stands in this chamber, while the other stands in that one. The life force of the first is transferred into the second."

"As simple as that?" Javier walked inside the opened chamber and reached for the twisted green harstone. It vibrated in his hand and left a warm sensation on his skin.

"Is it functional, Professor?" Onlor asked.

"The crystal is full of properties I don't understand. If you're asking me if it's possible this device can do what she claims, I'm sorry to say I can't determine that."

Onlor turned to his pair of guards standing by the entrance. Javier joined him and furrowed his brow.

"We need to see how this works," the expedition leader said.

"You want to put someone in there?" Javier asked.

"Two people. It won't work without two. Do you have a better idea, Professor?"

"You could let me study it." Javier grasped his scanner. "Something like this needs to be examined before we do anything stupid. You said yourself, we've got the finest minds here at our disposal. Let's use them."

Onlor rubbed his chin and ushered over his men. "You two, come here."

Undesignated Planet

Jason trudged through the long grass beyond the crashed *Bombay* and past the debris scattered across the forest floor, all the way back to the river. He walked the tightrope of the downed log and returned to where his adventure had started. The bubble representing his ride back to Plauvia sat in the same spot he'd left it. He stood in front of it, gazing at his rippled reflection, wondering how he'd explain to the others what had happened.

Just as he was about to take a step through, Kione materialized beside him. "You're going already?"

Jason pulled his foot back. "When I first arrived, it didn't seem like you wanted anything to do with me."

"I apologize for the way I came across." He smiled. "It has been nice seeing you again."

"I suppose neither of us expected our reunion to be under such circumstances."

The alien shook his head. "When I realized what I'd become, I thought the universe was my oyster. I could do almost anything, go almost anywhere, but when I found Doctor Tyrell, I discovered how wrong I was."

"Oh?"

"It's hard to explain. But I feel like I've cheated. Doctor Tyrell lived a remarkable life. And what did he get in return? To be buried beneath an alien world thousands of light years from his home."

"Yes, but because of that remarkable life his legacy will live on. You're part of that, Kione." Jason stepped closer to him. "The last thing Tyrell would've wanted is for you to feel sorry for him, or yourself for that matter."

Kione raised his eyebrows.

"There'd be a lot of people who'd love to be in the position you're in," Jason continued.

"Most of them wouldn't understand what it is to live like this."

Jason sighed "I apologize again for asking you to come back with me. I know I was out of line and—"

Kione put up his hand. "I don't disparage you for that."

A silence lingered between the pair.

"So, where are you going to go?" Jason asked. "The galaxy is a pretty big place."

Kione peered into the sky. "I once would have said that was true, but now I'm not so sure."

Jason went to place a hand on Kione's shoulder, but it passed through him like it had earlier.

"Good luck out there, Jason," his Retebu friend told him. "Say hello to everyone for me."

"Until next time?"

Jason approached the bubble, but just as he was about to step through, something grasped his shoulder.

He turned to Kione, whose face had changed from one of contentment to one of urgency. “What is it?” he asked.

“Danger!” Kione said. “Danger, everywhere!”

FORTY-THREE

Cargo Ship Argo

Aly gnashed down on her teeth, peering over Althaus's shoulder while more ships arrived through the gateway into Plauvia's orbit.

"What's the count now?" she asked.

"I'm reading nearly five hundred and fifty," he informed her, "made up of over eighty different designs."

"Who claimed the Alliance was dead and buried?" Aly walked over to her father at the helm, whose eyes hadn't left his monitors.

"You don't really believe this has anything to do with the Alliance, do you?" he said.

"Considering at least four of the races represented here have seceded, no, I don't. But it doesn't explain why they're here either."

"Perhaps they pissed someone off," Althaus said. "I doubt anyone's here for a party."

Aly glanced at the captain's chair. "This has to have something to do with Jason."

"If that's the case, maybe *he's* pissed someone off," Althaus quipped, laying the blame on his nephew.

Aly shot a glare at Jason's uncle, and he returned his attention to his scanners. She peered back through the viewport at the massive fleet swarming the orbit of Plauvia as even more ships joined them from the gateway. Too many questions bounced around in her head. Were they in fact looking at a new Alliance of some kind? If so, what were their intentions? And what did they want with Plauvia? Jason, however, was in the forefront of her mind. She wasn't about to give up on him. But she didn't know what to do.

"This isn't good..."

Everyone turned back to Althaus, and Aly rushed over to him.

He pointed at the scanners. "The fleet are breaking off into smaller groups and closing in on the planet's orbit."

Aly widened her eyes at the topographical image of the surface. "They're taking positions above the major populations centers. If we didn't know their true intentions before, we certainly do now."

Where are you down there, Jason?

Planet Zero

The two guards had been locked inside the Kalceni chambers for several minutes while the glow from the harstones produced an unnerving green radiance on the exterior of the ancient machines.

Javier turned to two more guards who'd arrived to take their place at the entrance of the laboratory. He wondered if they were thinking they'd be the next pair of guinea pigs to get sent through. Javier returned his gaze to Onlor, who watched on patiently. The obsessed Ulvekan didn't shirk his focus. Not even once.

A faint whirring sounded from each of the chambers until a significant reverberation vibrated through the floor, unsettling some dust from the ceiling. Then it abruptly stopped, and Onlor straightened his back, raising his eyebrows at the librarian.

"The procedure is complete," she said.

Onlor walked to the chamber and opened the door to find the first of his guards with his eyes closed. He reached in and motioned him out, but the man didn't move.

Javier scanned the alien and shook his head. "He's dead."

The guard face-planted on the ground with a thud, while Javier kneeled to his side to confirm his readings.

Onlor went over to the second chamber and yanked it ajar. Inside, the guard's eyes slowly opened, and he groggily staggered out, holding his temples.

"Can you hear me?" Onlor asked him, taking hold of him.

He didn't answer, and Javier joined Onlor, keeping him upright. "What's your name?"

The guard rubbed his forehead. "Minika?"

Onlor smiled at the fallen guard from the first chamber. "The transfer's complete."

The pair helped him down and sat him on the floor while he gathered his bearings. Javier scanned him and scratched his chin.

"What is it, Professor?" Onlor asked, no doubt noticing his intrigue.

"I've just done a basic brain scan of your guard."

"And?"

"It's confirmed something I've theorized for some time."

Javier tapped the scanner. "When Christian Nash was abducted at Nebula TPA-338, the Kalceni used him to host one of their consciousnesses. The Kalceni controlled him, but he was still there in some way. It was almost like a fusion of the two. This man has two noticeable brain waves. At least at the moment."

Onlor nodded. "I've read those reports, and I've liaised with other scientists who have come to the same conclusion. I believe it actually goes beyond that. Whenever a Kalceni consciousness jumps from one host to the other, they take with them part of the host they inhabited. Effectively every time they jump, they become more intelligent."

Javier placed his scanner on his belt. "What are we really doing here, Onlor? You've already lied to me more times that I can count now."

"Professor, please—"

"You've got no interest in the Kalceni at all, do you? Your fear that they might one day return is just fleeting."

"I'll admit a second invasion seems improbable."

"It was about this technology all along. You needed the Eternal Plan more than anything else." He didn't wait for Onlor to reply. "It's because of your Torvellan Syndrome, isn't it?"

Onlor didn't say anything for a moment, trying to find the words. He then laughed. "I should have known you'd crack the code eventually."

"The shaking. The coughing. The bloodshot eyes. All symptoms of the deadly disease known as the Torvellan Syndrome."

"I see you've been doing some reading on my people."

"It's what I do." Javier shrugged. "How long do you have to live?"

Onlor tugged at his collar and rounded the chambers. "Six months at the most."

Javier checked on the soldier to find him still struggling to come to terms with the transfer. "I suppose you see the Eternal Plan as your ticket from death to health."

The Ulvekan leaned against the nearest chamber. "I'll admit, initially my motives were quite selfish, but with everything that's been happening in the Alliance since the Kalceni attack, I've wondered if the Torvellan Syndrome was something of a godsend. Perhaps a sign to a higher calling."

Javier furrowed his brow. "I don't understand."

"Think about what I've said about the Alliance," Onlor continued. "Immeasurable damage has been done to a coalition of worlds that was once the height of civilization. It's been in a downward spiral for many years. The Kalceni attack was but the final nail in the coffin. Once it was steered by real leaders, but for too long it's been run by weak-minded fools who are now little more than paper-pushing bureaucrats."

Javier chuckled uncharacteristically, almost frightened where the conversation was going. "You think you could do better?"

"Me alone? No. The damage is too great. It would now take a goliath to restore order. Perhaps, though, with a bit of help..." Onlor glanced at the chambers. "...I could bring it back to its former glory and make it even greater."

Javier followed his gaze to the ancient technology. "You want to use this machine to become immortal?"

"Of course, being immortal is one bonus. Once a body has reached its end, all I'd have to do is move to another, but it's more than that. So much more."

"You want to feed off the knowledge of the host bodies you'll inhabit?"

"You've got it, Professor." Onlor tapped his head. "Why do you think I brought so many talented minds with me?"

Javier's jaw dropped as Onlor motioned for one of his guards. They promptly approached Javier and grabbed his shoulders tight.

"While it'll be a shame to say goodbye to this body and enter your weak human form, what I'll gain from your mind will be incalculable. And besides, it won't be for too long. There are so many other hosts that'll need to go through the process, too. Think what can be achieved from our melding of experiences."

Javier struggled under the grip of the guards. They pushed him inside the second chamber, and Onlor stepped in front of him.

"Don't worry, Professor, this shouldn't take long."

Undesignated Planet

"Danger? What are you talking about?"

Jason looked at his friend in puzzlement as Kione darted his eyes around him.

The alien pulled his hand off him after ensuring he wasn't going to enter the bubble. "I can't explain it."

Jason shook his head. "Why does that not surprise me?"

"You have to understand, there's more happening out there than you can know right now."

"Of that, I have no doubt."

"Your human quips aren't helping."

"Sorry." Jason put his hands up in surrender. "What do you plan to do?"

Kione bit his bottom lip and raised a finger. A beam shot from it and immersed the bubble. The beam and the bubble soon dissipated and disappeared into nothingness.

Jason craned his head. "How am I supposed to get back to Plauvia?"

"Plauvia is the last place you want to go right now." Kione put out his hand. "Are you ready?"

"Ready, for what?"

"You need to trust me."

Jason looked down at the outstretched hand of his friend. While they'd certainly had disagreements in the past, he couldn't ever fault the man for being untrustworthy. Jason gave him his hand, and a fuzziness ran up his arm. Their green surroundings disappeared until both of them found themselves surrounded by darkness.

FORTY-FOUR

Planet Zero

Javier banged on the door inside the chamber and tried to push it open, battering his shoulder against it. But it wouldn't budge. He didn't have the strength he used to, and even if he did, he doubted he could break the latching mechanism.

Above, the green light from the harstone crystal pulsated over him while it whirred inside its housing. The chamber vibrated, and the reverberation from the moving parts of the ancient machine jangled every bone in his body. Not wanting to become a victim like the poor guards who were forced into the chambers, he yanked the mobile holographic device from his pocket and slammed it into the door.

Again and again, he struck it.

But the door didn't give.

The whining from the crystal intensified, and Javier put his hands over his ears.

Then a voice addressed him over the din.

"Hello, Professor."

Javier pulled his hands away and stared around his greenly bathed confines.

"Can you hear me?" the voice called out again.

"Onlor?" Javier said, recognizing the voice. The sound was distant, but also right there with him.

"I can feel you near me, Professor."

Javier too felt the Ulvekan close. Much too close for his liking. He put his hands on the door and closed his eyes, trying to ignore him.

"You can't push me away, Professor. You must let go. Soon we will be one, and with your help I'll be on my rightful path to restoring order to the Alliance."

"I won't let that happen," Javier shot back.

His head tingled around his temples, and his brain pulsated, as if a migraine were jackhammering away inside skull.

"We're so close now."

Javier yelled out in horror as not only the words of Onlor appeared in his mind, but also his memories.

The darkness around Jason subsided, but instead of arriving somewhere he might have been familiar with, he found himself in a dimly lit room, which looked like it could collapse at any moment.

Before he had a chance to ask where he was, two

alien guards in Company uniforms approached with their rifles aimed at him. His instincts immediately came to the fore, and he fly-kicked a gun from one guard's hands.

The other guard cracked Jason across the head with his own weapon and sent him flying to the floor. "Identify yourself now!" he yelled at him.

Jason raised his hands as the guard closed on him.

Then a flash of light shimmered on the other side of the room, and Kione appeared. The guard turned, while the other picked up his rifle and joined him. The pair shuffled toward Kione with their weapons pointed at him. But, before they could utter a word, Kione simply waved at them, and they launched through the air and slammed into the wall, scattering onto the floor.

Jason pulled himself up and approached the two upright containers at the center of the room, making a strange whirring sound while glowing a radiant green. "What the hell are these things?"

Kione walked to the first door and swung it open. A body fell out of the chamber and tumbled into his arms. Kione let him down on the floor slowly, and Jason helped him roll the alien over onto his back. He recognized the alien immediately.

"An Ulvekan? Is he dead?" Jason asked, trying to find a pulse in the lanky being's arm.

"Yes." Kione nodded, and another figure appeared from behind the chambers. Jason pulled himself back up as the semi-transparent being moved toward them.

"A Retebu!" he gasped. "A Guardian?"

The female stared at Kione with her mouth agape.

"Wrong on both counts." Kione stood and walked around her while she remained in front of the two containers. "It's Kalceni." He placed his hand through her. "A hologram, too."

"But she looks just like you," Jason said.

"That's because at one point the Kalceni and the Retebu were once the same." Kione waved at the hologram, and it shimmered from existence. "A history lesson for later."

He moved to the other container and reached for the door, pulling it off its hinges. Another body dropped from it into Kione's arms.

"Professor Petit!" Jason shouted.

The groggy man's eyes were closed, and he muttered some indistinct words under his breath. Kione placed him on the floor while Jason put a hand on his shoulder.

"Professor, can you hear me?" he said, but the elder statesman of Earth's science community didn't answer. "Kione, what's going on here?"

His Retebu friend motioned toward the containers. "This place was once the Kalceni home world. These chambers are their first attempt at achieving immortality."

Jason stared up at the ancient technology. "This is the same process Christian Nash went through when he was abducted by them?"

Kione nodded, and the professor's eyes fluttered and slowly opened. Petit looked up at them for a moment, as if wondering where he was. He then tried to heave himself up, but Jason kept him flat with his caring but firm hands.

A smile appeared on the professor's weathered face. "You're the last two people I expected to see."

"Are you okay?" Jason asked him.

Petit put out his hand and pointed to something beyond them. Jason followed his finger where a scanner lay on the floor. He grabbed it and handed it to the professor.

Petit held it over himself and stared down at the readings, breathing a sigh of relief. "The transfer was interrupted before it could take hold."

Jason checked over the dead body of who he suspected had tried to implant his consciousness into Petit. He wanted to ask so many questions, but Kione placed a hand on his shoulder and stood.

"There's much more to do," he said.

"There is?" Jason raised his eyebrows, and darkness again fell over them.

Cargo Ship Argo

"They're getting ready to fire."

Aly grasped the back of her father's chair at Althaus's call from the systems station. She desperately wanted to know what to do. Jason seemed to always have answers to the most impossible of scenarios. Why didn't she?

"Here they go!" Althaus said.

Her father reached out for her hand, and she took it, finding some comfort in the man who had raised her. Then the fireworks began as the ships in orbit launched their arsenals against the major population centers of Plauvia. She closed her eyes and thought about Jason. Somewhere he was on the surface along with the tens of millions of Plauvians who called the doomed planet home. She wanted to collapse to the deck in a ball, but her dad's grip kept her from falling.

"Are we picking up any evacuation crafts leaving the planet?" Doctor Tai asked.

Althaus shook his head. "There's nothing."

"Nothing at all?" Aly said.

"I suppose they figure, what's the point? No evacuation would make it through all that, anyway."

Aly grabbed at her chest. "Jason..."

"I'm not going anywhere just yet, Aly."

Aly straightened her back and craned her neck at the voice. She spun around, along with everyone else, to find three figures materializing at the rear of the bridge.

Jason, Professor Petit, and Kione all appeared from nothingness. For several moments she tried to understand what had just happened, until she finally ran over to Jason and wrapped her arms around him. "I didn't think I'd ever see you again."

"That makes two of us."

She pulled herself away from him and kissed him on his lips. "How's this possible?"

Jason glanced at Professor Petit who made his way to Doctor Tai while Kione stood near the hatchway existing as if he were a ghost or spirit of some kind. "Beats me."

FORTY-FIVE

Jason desperately wanted to let everyone in on what had happened since his journey to Plauvia and beyond, but he didn't know where to begin. Besides, there were greater problems at hand. He thought about Mirin, Brukan, and the others he'd met on the planet. They were a complex people who cared deeply for the state of the galaxy. They certainly didn't deserve to die from the hellfire being released down on top of them.

He walked over to Althaus and checked the scanners at the carnage taking place before them. While Plauvia's attackers had no weapon ship at their disposal, they were doing immense damage to the surface of the planet.

"Why are they doing this?" Aly looked at Jason as if he had the answer. Eventually everyone turned their attention to Kione.

The alien stepped to the center of the bridge next to the captain's chair. "The Plauvians represent the last vestige of order. With the Alliance splintered, chaos is now on the precipice of spreading throughout the galaxy. Only one thing stands in its way."

Jason nodded. "The word of the Firstborns..."

"They are the final remnants of the Retebu still in existence. Not including myself, of course. Those that want to see a final end to order see it as their last obstacle."

"I'm reading instability occurring beneath the planet's crust," Althaus informed everyone. "The tectonic plates are being shifted from all the weapon fire. Earthquakes are registering across the surface, and volcanic activity is erupting at sporadic locations."

Aly stared at the readings. "They're literally shaking the planet apart."

Jason walked up to Kione. "This isn't what the Retebu wanted. You know that, don't you?"

The cogs inside Kione's hyper-evolved mind appeared to turn, and he reached out, placing a hand on Jason's shoulder. The alien smiled at him. "You've been a good friend, Jason."

"This is goodbye again for a while, isn't it?" Jason said.

Kione didn't answer him, instead meeting everyone's gaze. The thinnest of smiles appeared, and he shimmered from existence as if he hadn't even been there. The strange sensation on Jason's shoulder disappeared, and he sat in the captain's chair. Silence permeated around him as Plauvia's attackers continued to pummel the peaceful world below.

But then the energy weapons creating a haze of fireworks subsided.

"We've got some activity," Kevin said from the helm.

"The fleet is moving away from the planet," Althaus confirmed.

"I guess they don't want to be around just in case it blows." Jason rested his chin in his hand while the attacking fleet maneuvered from Plauvia's orbit like a swarm of locusts fleeing their nest.

The *Argo* rocked from side to side from the thruster activity of the huge number of ships maneuvering by them. Once they cleared, the desert world beyond sat amongst the stars silently. It was a pale comparison of what it had looked like when Mirin initially took Jason there. The green areas near the sea were gone, and the white fluffy clouds were replaced with dark-gray volcanic ash. Beneath, he could only imagine the golden sands being turned into glass.

"I'd suggest we follow those ships and get out of here," Althaus advised. "If that planet goes to kingdom come, we won't have time to flee."

Jason tapped his fingers on the arm of his chair while Kevin swiveled around and stared at him expectantly, with his hand firmly planted on the thrusters ready for the order.

"No, we'll stay here," Jason decided.

"Are you mad!" Althaus blurted out.

Jason chuckled. He wondered how it was possible to find something so amusing at such a moment.

"If that planet blows..." Althaus turned to Kevin.

"Hold our position," Jason reiterated to his helmsman before he could utter a word.

Aly joined his side and put her hand on the arm of his chair. He took it and wrapped his fingers around it. Then they waited.

And waited.

Plauvia transformed from yellow to gray, appearing more like a desolate gaseous moon than a planet with the ability to support life.

But it didn't explode.

Jason eyed the system stations. "What are you reading over there?"

Althaus shook his head. "Nothing. The scanners can't penetrate the cloud layer."

Jason scratched at his stubble, and suddenly the gray volcanic ash started to diminish. Little by little, the darkness filling Plauvia's atmosphere lightened and then disappeared.

Aly unclasped herself from Jason and hurried over to the systems station to check over the incoming readings. "I don't believe it. The earthquakes. They're stopping. The tectonic plates are settling back into their original position. Whatever volcanic activity there was, is vanishing."

"Can you get me a topographic scan of one of their cities?" Jason asked.

Althaus prodded at his console, and live footage from the surface above the modest metropolises appeared on Jason's command station. Leveled buildings formed from the rubble and rebuilt themselves. Around the cities, the sparse greenery reappeared, and the dark-blue water became crystal clear once again.

"Well, I'll be damned," he muttered. "So much for magic fairy dust."

He stood and walked past Kevin, taking in the breadth of the planet through the viewport. Never had a desert world looked so beautiful.

Althaus's console beeped, and he checked over his monitor. "It seems the attacking fleet has figured out what's going on. They're returning to orbit."

Just as before, but in reverse, the locusts came back, blacking out the sun and taking up positions above Plauvia.

"They must wonder what the hell happened." Aly went to her father's side. "I'd love to be a fly on the wall on one of those ships right now."

"No need," Althaus said. "They're preparing to fire again!"

They all gazed out at the first ship readying to attack. It extended its wings into an aggressive position and readied its weapon batteries. Several orange wisps of energy fired out from its emitters and burst toward the surface, but instead of the energy beams piercing the planet's atmosphere, they boomeranged, striking their own hull and obliterating them.

"Whoa!" Jason dropped his jaw as other vessels made the same attempt. Again, their fire simply ricocheted off the invisible shield surrounding the planet and either destroyed, or badly damaged them.

"Over twenty ships have been blown to smithereens." Althaus shook his head at the scanner. "At least another thirty have been crippled."

"Well, would you look at that?" Kevin gestured through the viewport as the enormous fleet scattered beyond Plauvia's orbit. The gateway activated, and they all streamed into it, returning to wherever they'd come from.

Aly approached Jason, and he wrapped his arms around her waist, but just before he could kiss her, an alert sounded from the systems station.

Jason rolled his eyes. "Now what?"

"We're receiving a commlink from the surface," Althaus said.

"Put it on." Jason led Aly to the command station, and they both peered down at the incoming transmission. Both Mirin and Brukan appeared on the monitor.

"Jason," the cleric began. *"You have done our world an immense service."*

"I—"

"Not only that but you've righted a wrong in the galaxy and returned it on a path toward peace."

Jason shook his head. "I didn't do any of this. It was—"

"We know," Mirin interjected. *"But if it wasn't for you reaching out to the Guardian, he may never have come."*

Jason glanced back at the rear of the bridge where Kione had stood and wondered where his friend was now.

Or where he was going next.

Hopefully he'll be happy.

FORTY-SIX

"That's remarkable!"

Javier shook his head as Susan walked from one end of the *Argo's* rec room to the other, completely unencumbered. She didn't even put out a hand to clamp on to anything to keep her balance. A giddiness flowed through her she hadn't experienced for a very long time.

She sat across from her friend at the chess table, and they both peered through the viewport at the trans-space corridor surrounding the *Argo*. They'd enjoyed a few days of celebration on Plauvia with the locals before Jason decided it was time to head home. While visiting the desert world was fun, there was something homely about being back aboard the rickety old cargo ship again.

"So, what's the next move for Doctor Tai?" Javier asked her. "You've been keeping yourself busy for a while now. Any chance of slowing down?"

She put her hands on her thighs, feeling the sensation of her fingertips on top of them. "Now that I've got these back, nobody will be able to stop me. Depending on what happens with the Alliance, I wouldn't mind staying out here."

Javier smiled. "I couldn't think of anything more appropriate."

"What about you?" she asked him. "How are you feeling with everything that happened on the Kalceni home world?"

He scratched his head. "Let's just say I'm not keen on returning there anytime soon."

She eyed him with a crooked brow. "You said that about the base at Kappa-Magellan, too."

He chuckled nervously. "I guess I did."

"Are you going to return to Hokkaido?"

He gazed past her into nothingness. "No. I think I might head back to TIAS. If they'll have me. While my experience with Onlor and this expedition won't be something I'll remember too fondly, it has taught me that even though I've lived more of my life than not, I've still got plenty to give. Being holed up in that little tree-house in Hokkaido can wait. I'd rather give it my all before my light is completely extinguished."

She smiled and reached for her glass of water next to the chess set. "To giving it our all before our light's extinguished."

Jason tossed and turned. He'd been unable to get a wink of sleep ever since leaving Plauvia. He couldn't remember the last time he'd gotten a chance to rest his eyes since the current craziness had begun.

Jason glanced at Aly who was fast asleep on the pillow beside him. There was a calmness about her, even in slumber. He knew how much she second-guessed herself, but she was so much more than she could know. She was a remarkable soul. One he was glad to be sharing his life with.

As quietly as he could, he pulled the sheets from himself and slipped into a shirt and pants. He opened the door to their quarters and quickly closed it up, blocking any light from coming in. He made his way to the elevator and directed it to C Deck. There he strode across the cargo bay, to find Kevin and Althaus up the other end looking inside a maintenance junction.

Althaus had been given his reprieve from his crutches and stood that little more upright. For a moment he stared at the two men, and they appeared as they had when he was a child. Tall, strong, and young. The galaxy was their oyster.

He left them on their own and walked through the airlock to the *Julieanne* which they'd retrieved from Plauvia.

He took a seat at the helm and placed his legs underneath the console. But something obstructed his feet. Jason reached under and pulled out his father's guitar, placing it on his lap. He chuckled and twanged at the strings, finding his attempt at creating anything reasonably coherent as amusing as ever. He plonked the instrument beside him and leaned back, closing his eyes.

Then something clunked behind him, and he reopened them, swiveling around to find the source of the disturbance. There in the darkness, a huddled figure sat in the corner.

Jason picked up the guitar, the only object resembling a weapon within sight, and moved into the rear compartment of the *Julieanne.* He prodded at the controls on the bulkhead and illuminated the interior of the transport pod, bathing it in a bright light.

Jason dropped the instrument by his side and did a double take. "Kione?"

His friend took his head out from between his legs, and his eyes slowly opened, adjusting to the brightness. Jason reached out for his hand, and the Retebu took it. It wasn't until he started pulling the alien to his feet that he discovered what had happened.

"I can touch you?" he said. "I can't see through you anymore. You're solid."

"Flesh and bone." Kione rubbed his head and sat on a fold-out seat.

"What's happened to you?" Jason asked.

"My powers are gone."

Jason raised his eyebrows. "You mean you're not an evolved Retebu anymore? You're the Kione I knew before you came into contact with the sphere?"

"That's right."

"How's that possible?"

"Because when one has the abilities I had, they get to choose what to do with them," Kione told him.

"Wait a minute." Jason rubbed his temples. "So,

you're saying you did this deliberately. What you did on Plauvia didn't exhaust you in some way?"

Kione chuckled. "It doesn't work like that."

"You chose to become a mere mortal again?"

His friend nodded.

Jason pulled out the seat beside him. "Why?"

Kione sighed. "Because once you're immortal there is nothing else. You can do and see anything you want. Once there is no challenge, there is no point."

"But with that power you've made a difference. Ever since the defeat over those that attacked on Plauvia, every member of the Alliance is returning to the table. There is hope it might become whole again."

"And now the ball is in their court. This Guardian will no longer be there to look over them. It's time for the younger races of the galaxy to figure it out for themselves."

"So, the book is closed?" Jason smiled. "What does that mean for you? Without the ability to simply click your fingers to whisk yourself to any part of the universe anymore, your journey from here will be a much different one."

"I suppose I'll have to explore the old-fashioned way." Kione leaned back. "You don't know of a ship who has an opening in their crew, do you?"

Jason gestured to the airlock, and they stepped through to the *Argo*. "I may just have a ship in mind."

A MESSAGE FROM ROBERT

There's nothing more I enjoy than building relationships with my readers. You can join my Reader's Club for news on my latest releases, receive exclusive bonus content, get free ebooks, and be the first to know about special deals.

Join today by visiting www.robertcjames.com

Milton Keynes UK
Ingram Content Group UK Ltd.
UKHW011809060324
438908UK00017B/2

9 780645 138757